DARK OBSESSION

OTHER BOOKS BY EDWARD GLOVER

THE HERZBERG TRILOGY

The Music Book

A young English woman, on the run from her father, and a retired Prussian military officer sent to England by King Frederick the Great are plunged into the London demi-monde and a pursuit across Europe in search of fulfilment. The young woman's music book bears witness to what unfolds.

Fortune's Sonata

English by birth, Prussian by marriage, rebellious by nature, the beautiful Arabella von Deppe steers her family through turbulent historical times in this thrilling story of love and loss, betrayal and revenge, ambition and beliefs, friendship and fate. With music as her inspiration and a murderer as her friend, she proves a worthy adversary of Fortune as she weathers winds beyond her control.

A Motif of Seasons

Two powerful 19th-century English and Prussian families are still riven by the consequences of an ancestral marriage – one that bequeathed venomous division, rivalry and hatred. Three beautiful women – each ambitious and musically gifted – seek to break these inherited shackles of betrayal, revenge and cruelty in their pursuit of sexual freedom and love. But the past proves a formidable and vicious opponent.

* * *

The Executioner's House

Germany, October 1946. The Nuremburg war crimes tribunal has just ended. Major Richard Fortescue, previously part of the British prosecution team, is returning to London when he encounters Karin Eilers, a young German woman with a dark past. Against the backdrop of war-devastated Berlin and the continuing search for former Nazis, their brief affair and a mysterious black notebook make them unwitting pawns in a deadly game of intrigue and betrayal played by British and Soviet intelligence. What wartime secrets will the notebook unravel? Who else will become a victim of the battle for its possession?

The Lute Player

Mystery, obsession, rage, joy, demons, death, secrets and a lute. All to be found on Johannes' journey – a father's search, an artist's mission, a lost soul's quest – where nothing, especially Khadra the lute player, is ever quite what it seems. Venture beyond the borders of the Herzberg trilogy and *The Executioner's House* to an intensely personal landscape in which fantasy, fable and metaphysics overlay ancient civilisations, and threads of history, music and art weave through a vividly conjured seeker's story.

Dark Obsession

EDWARD GLOVER

Published by The Oak House
High Street, Thornham, Norfolk PE36 6LY

Cover photograph by Quang Nguyen Vinh

ISBN: 978-0-9929551-5-1

Suspicion always haunts the guilty mind
William Shakespeare

For the first time he perceived that if you want to keep a secret you must also hide it from yourself. You must know all the while that it is there, but until it is needed you must never let it emerge into your consciousness in any shape that could be given a name.
George Orwell

I have little left in myself – I must have you. The world may laugh – may call me absurd, selfish – but it does not signify. My very soul demands you: it will be satisfied, or it will take deadly vengeance on its frame.
Charlotte Brontë

PERIOD FRENCH MAP OF INDOCHINA

CONTENTS

PART ONE

Obsession

PROLOGUE

It was never meant to be like this. It should never have happened. But it did.

Now, in the realm of the damned, comes the reckoning and the inevitable consequences of abhorrent actions.

CHAPTER ONE

The River

It began so simply, on a liquid sun-steeped day – late afternoon, I recall – in the family's summer residence by the river. I got up from the piano, where I'd been playing a Chopin sonata, to stand in the open veranda doorway. The trees on the far bank and those on the hillside beyond were cloaked in an undulating deep-gold lucent light. An occasional warm breeze brushed the lace curtains. There was no sound in the sultry laziness of the approaching evening. Then I saw her. She sat beneath a parasol in a skiff moving effortlessly along the river, her hand trailing in the water. Her female companion was rowing, her featherlike strokes barely rippling the surface. The boat – vermilion orange in the sunlight – was vivid against the cobalt blue of reflected sky, the sunshine seeming to dissolve the line between hull and water, causing a shimmering interlacing of colours.

She was young, in a white, full-sleeved dress, her long dark hair bound by a purple ribbon beneath a white wide-brimmed hat with a matching purple band. Her companion, a little older, was dressed in pale yellow, her copper hair pinned beneath a boater decorated with flowers. I strained to hear what they were saying but their voices were too muted. As the skiff drew near, another puff of breeze tugged at the curtains framing the doorway in which I stood. I stepped back so as not to be seen but my movement must have caught her attention. She looked up. I fleetingly saw her face, radiant with happiness. She smiled. I half raised my hand in salutation, to which there was no response. A moment later the boat was gone, past the weeping willow, leaving no wake, no trace.

For the rest of that day and for days after, I could not erase her features from my mind. I sought a local artist to capture her image from my description, but hard though I tried to describe her face his sketches could not depict what I had seen. All I could do was record in my diary the day I had seen her.

> *Sunday the 22nd of August 1875. I saw today an enchanting young woman on the river, bathed in golden sunlight. Who she was I do not know. I cannot remove her from my mind. There she is indelibly etched. I must try to find her, to see her face again, to know her name, to make her acquaintance if that were possible.*

Later the same year, I saw her again at the Opéra Comique in Paris, while scanning the audience at a performance of Bizet's *Carmen*, the premiere of which had scandalised its first audiences that spring, to see who I might know. She was seated in a box on the other side of the proscenium. Though my view was partially obscured, I was certain it was her, just as beautiful as she had been in the boat.

To her left was an older, well-dressed woman wrapped in a fur stole and beyond her a grey-haired man in white tie. Perhaps they were her parents. To her right was a young man, a little older than her and fussy-looking, preoccupied with his opera glasses to ascertain, like me, who from high society was present. I observed her closely. Her hair was pinned up in a chignon beneath a small feathered hat. Her gown was dark purple, almost off-the-shoulder in style, with the sleeves revealing white lace around the cuffs. She leaned forwards to catch sight of the orchestra as it entered the pit. Judging by the wonderment on her face, I surmised this might be her first visit to the opera. She suddenly looked up and across in my direction, perhaps aware I was gazing at her. Yes! I was convinced. It was indeed her. For a moment, our eyes locked. She smiled, as she did in the boat. Whether she recognised me, or her smile was directed at someone else, I could not say.

The lights dimmed, the overture began. Not even the rising curtain and the drama of the first act could subdue the fermenting obsession that had been reawakened by seeing her. More than ever, I had to find out who she was, to make her acquaintance, to touch her hand.

In the first and second intervals, she and those with her remained in their box. But as the curtain fell on the third act, she stood to follow her companions out. I mingled amidst the clamour for champagne in the foyer, searching for her, but she was nowhere to be seen, even as the audience slowly filed back into the auditorium for the last act.

My behaviour displeased my companion.

"Émile! What is the matter with you? You seem so distracted. You've hardly spoken to me all evening. Please give me your attention. You invited me to accompany you here but have entirely ignored my presence. Your mind seems to be elsewhere. This is most unlike you and it is certainly not the way to win a young woman's heart. Indeed, Maman and Papa have asked me if they have said something to offend you. If not, being silent is surely not the way to behave. If you're tired of me, please say so and I too will turn my attention, and affections, elsewhere. I assure you there is no shortage of suitors for my hand."

"Monique, I beg you to forgive me. I do not mean to slight you or your esteemed parents. I've been preoccupied at the Ministry in recent days. The thought of departing Paris before long, leaving you, and of all the preparations I have to do – these have been foremost in my mind. My lack of conversation this evening is of course intolerable. I assure you it won't happen again. I promise to make full amends for my discourtesy."

"I'm pleased to hear it. I warn you that I shall do whatever is necessary to ensure you keep your word."

She gripped my arm tightly as we followed her parents back to the box. As the curtain rose, she whispered that there was one inarguable way for me to show my undying commitment to her.

"Tonight, after supper, let us slip away to your apartment. You have said many times that I've turned your world upside down. If that is the case, show me by making love to me. I expect no less."

"Monique, you scandalise me. You have let this opera go to your head!"

"Émile, don't be so pompous. It doesn't suit you. I am no Carmen. The stories of your *amours* are well known in the social circles in which my family and yours mix. I will not accept any excuses. You know what you have to do."

I smiled, as she pressed her heel down on my shoe.

As we stood outside the theatre afterwards, waiting for the carriage to take us to supper at La Tour d'Argent – a restaurant allegedly dating back to the sixteenth century but whose food I found overpraised – I saw her again in the mêlée, closer this time, stepping into a coach further along the pavement. She was assisted by her male companion, her beau, perhaps. As she waved goodbye to the others who had been in their box, she suddenly turned and looked in my direction, this time clearly without any sign of recognition. Not deterred, I nodded. She half smiled but, as before, whether at me or someone else, I did not know. In an instant, she was gone.

My gesture did not pass unnoticed.

"Émile! There you go again – not paying attention," Monique scolded. "To whom did you nod?"

"Someone I thought I recognised from the Ministry. But I was mistaken."

After an execrable supper, we managed to escape her weary parents on the pretext of a late-night tour of the city centre. In the privacy of my apartment and with more champagne, Monique kissed me, pressing her body against mine.

"Émile, it is time to do your penance. Show how much you care for me."

I was cornered. She was striking, poised and alluring. But was she truly the woman I wanted as my wife?

As I undid her gown, unlaced her corset, and she removed her slip and unpinned her hair – that ravishing hair – I could not but surrender to this formidable seductress. But even as I placed her on my bed, all I could think of was the girl in the skiff, the girl at the opera. If only it was her I had undressed, if only it was her I was about to make love to. Monique held me tightly as we lay pressed together. Once I had extinguished the bedside candle, she would not see my conflict. I realised then that I had become obsessed by a young woman I had never met, whose name I did not know, whom I had seen only twice.

The next morning, on my way to the Ministry, I went to the Louvre to enlist the help of one of the promising young artists who are always to be found there copying masterpieces. Despite his talent, however, the one I chose could not capture what I described any more successfully than the painter in Provence. Later, I went to a studio that taught life drawing in the hope I might see a model who would remind me of her, but to no avail. I even attempted to sketch her myself. Increasingly frustrated, some evenings I lied to Monique, claiming I was detained at my desk in order to wander the streets in the forlorn hope that I might catch sight of her. It was no use. Perhaps she didn't exist. Perhaps she was just a figment of my imagination. I should forget her. But however hard I tried, I couldn't.

A week or so later, ever more driven by the urge to find her, it occurred to me there was possibly another way. Through a reliable contact I enlisted the services of a former detective to trace the occupants of the box that night at the Opéra Comique. It was a perilous step – I would be revealing my obsession to someone else I did not know – but I had to do it. Chief Inspector Hector Deveaux accepted my commission, agreeing not to disclose the task I had given him to anyone, on pain of death. His fee was not cheap – the price, he said, of strict confidentiality – but for me it was affordable, a financial trifle. The son of a wealthy father still open-handed despite his offspring's independence (through both income and inclination), I had the money, reputation and connections to secure whatever I wanted. Besides, while I might be driven by an obsession, it was ultimately merely a game to me, albeit the stakes were high. That night, after an evening with Monique and with her once more in my bed, I could not sleep. My conscience told me that the instruction I had given Deveaux was morally wrong – I was betraying Monique, making a pawn of an unsuspecting young woman – but I was determined I would not withdraw it.

For a week or more I heard nothing. Becoming impatient, I contacted him, but he told me not to pester him. He was on the case and if he had information that he considered would be helpful he would let me know without delay. Until then I should go about my normal business. Yet that was proving increasingly difficult. Though I tried hard to be attentive to Monique and to my work at the Ministry of Foreign Affairs, I could not get the image of that beautiful young woman out of my mind. She haunted me throughout the day. At night, I was unable to sleep. I imagined speaking to her, kissing her, holding her, making love to her. She had become an overwhelming obsession, enslaving me – me, the independent, influential, insouciant Émile de Beaudreau. I contacted Deveaux once more but again he rebuffed me, insisting I should be patient.

A day or so later the Minister took me aside. He said that, with my posting to Berlin now almost certain, it would be appropriate for me to arrive in Germany as a married man. Well briefed, he was aware of my liaison with Monique d'Aurevalle and of her father's position in Parisian high society as an extremely successful – and manipulative – industrialist and entrepreneur.

"I'm convinced you will flourish in your career. Your skill, talent and connections will serve both you and our diplomatic mission in Berlin well at this difficult time in our country's relationship with the German Reich. There is much to do to overcome the shame of our defeat at Sedan and the proclamation of the German Empire at Versailles."

I nodded, wondering how much longer I would have to listen.

"Of course, it is not for me to tell you what to do in your personal affairs but I suggest that it would be advantageous to cement your forthcoming appointment as a married man. It would also put paid to the rumours, which I am sure are unfounded, about your affairs with other women."

He looked at me expectantly but, though inwardly seething at such remarks from a politician of limited repute, I said nothing.

"Mademoiselle d'Aurevalle is a most attractive, intelligent and persuasive young woman," the Minister continued, "the latter quality inherited from her mother. If it is your intention to marry her, as I hear it is, I recommend you announce your intention without delay. The marriage would scotch not only the rumours to which I have referred but also their possible exploitation in Berlin. I'm sure you would agree, Monsieur de Beaudreau."

"Thank you, Minister, for your advice. I will bear it in mind."

"Good," he replied, "though I expect you to do more than bear my words in mind. I trust you will take them into account."

I nodded again. Being a lawyer like my father, and schooled in the subtleties of language, I was well aware of the semantic distinction between the two formulations he had uttered. After some remaining pleasantries, I took my leave.

In the spring of 1876, I married Monique d'Aurevalle at the Church of Saint-Sulpice. She was radiant on that day, and her father and mother also beamed with delight that their treasured daughter had established a powerful union between two leading Parisian families, one of business and one of law. The day before the wedding, I received a note from Deveaux saying he had been unable to identify the occupants of the Opéra Comique box as there had been a last-minute resale of the tickets. He would continue his efforts but, for the moment, his primary preoccupation was a less trivial case. Unsure of his commitment, and despite my imminent marriage, I urged him in the strongest of terms to continue, reminding him of the need to resolve the matter before my departure from Paris and promising to increase his financial reward if he discovered the young woman's identity. The obsession's tight grip remained.

We arrived in Trouville for our honeymoon on Easter Monday, the 17th of April.

The destination was Monique's choice – glamorous villas, a wide sandy beach and a casino where she could display her rich assortment of evening gowns. The weather was unseasonably warm, providing abundant opportunities for afternoon walks on the promenade and beach. The town was patronised by a throng of haute bourgeoisie not to my particular taste. Besides, I had stayed there before, seducing a woman in a shabby hotel in one of the back streets. Making a supreme effort, I tolerated the daily social routine, the meaningless chatter, for my wife's sake, but each day was difficult to bear. However hard I tried I could not dislodge the image that had wormed its way deep into my psyche. At night when I made love to my wife I imagined only that I was doing so to the nameless young woman. I hoped that before long, once I was in Berlin and preoccupied with embracing our intolerable enemy, I might finally force her out of my mind.

One afternoon not long before our honeymoon ended, Monique and I walked along the promenade overlooking the beach, as we had done almost every day since our arrival. And I saw her, coming towards us, illuminated by the sun. I knew it was her – the girl I had first seen in the skiff and then at the opera.

Dressed in a long, elegant, white summer dress that ruffled in the gentle breeze and carrying a large-brimmed straw hat, she was strolling along the beach below. Her hair was pinned in a loose bun. She was accompanied by an older woman in a matching white dress, wearing a similar hat from which trailed a long white veil, and holding an open parasol, also white. I quickened my pace, much to Monique's irritation, to get closer to the two women as they approached. Yes. It was indeed her. Her face and profile were unmistakable. They passed by without looking up at the promenade. Pretending I had dropped a handkerchief I persuaded Monique to retrace our steps. Walking quickly, we soon overtook the two women and after a short distance I encouraged Monique to descend to the beach, ostensibly to look for the handkerchief but in truth to be nearer to the approaching young woman and her companion, still deep in conversation, oblivious to those around them.

As they passed by on this occasion, I got a closer sight of her. She was unblemishedly young and truly beautiful. From their similar height and slenderness I concluded that her companion was most likely her mother. She did not look at me, suddenly preoccupied with something she had seen in the distance. Monique and I walked on but after a while I said that as the handkerchief seemed irretrievably lost it was time to return to the hotel. As we turned, I looked for the two women in their distinctive dresses but they had vanished, their footsteps lost in the many on the sand. While we walked, I decided, in the absence of any information from Deveaux, to give the young woman the name of Marie Desanges – Mary, our lady of the angels.

The following day, our last in Trouville, Monique and I walked once more along the promenade but there was no sign of Marie on the beach, or in the casino that night.

Not long after our return to Paris, the Under-Secretary asked to see me. He informed me that my intended assignment in Berlin had been cancelled and that instead I was being posted to assist the French administrator in Cochinchina, where my abilities would be put to better use. That evening, I discovered my change of destination had been engineered by Monique's father, on account of his growing commercial interests in the region. I could scarcely disguise my displeasure, indeed anger. I had always been master of my own destiny. Moreover, a greater distance would now separate me from the woman with whom I had become so obsessed and whose identity I was yet to uncover.

Monique came to the Gare de Lyon to wave farewell, excited that within some three months she would follow me on the long journey east. We kissed and after her last tender embrace I boarded the night train to Marseille, my mind in turmoil.

The train slipped out of the station into the grey rain-swept dusk. Paris was soon left far behind, replaced by the prospect of interminable night. I looked at my sombre reflection in the window, beside it the luminous face of Marie. It was her I longed for, not Monique. I had become trapped in a marriage I was already beginning to regret, a union I was convinced would dissolve into bitterness and rancour.

I ate a few mouthfuls of the elaborate supper an attendant brought to my compartment before pushing the tray away. I had no appetite. I leafed through some papers a Ministry clerk had thrust into my hand shortly before Monique and I said goodbye. Amongst what seemed to me to be tedious, inconsequential items was a wax-sealed letter marked *Strictly Personal*. I looked at the sender's name on the reverse, recognising it immediately. I tore the envelope open. Inside was a note in neat handwriting.

> *To my client,*
> *After prolonged and careful enquiries, I have established beyond reasonable doubt that the young woman you described to me is Anne-Sophie Courcel, aged 19. She is from a well-respected Normandy family, whose ancestry may be traced back to the ancient dukedom of Burgundy, with whom she lives at Le Port-Marly, on the outskirts of Paris. I have good reason to believe she is due to marry, but I have not yet verified the identity of the young man concerned.*
> *Please send further instructions if you wish me to continue.*
> *Deveaux*

At last I knew her name. I felt a frisson of excitement. Now I had her within my reach, I would not let her go. I would endeavour, with Deveaux's connivance, to block the intended match by whatever means necessary. This would be a game I would win. She would be mine. After all, I was used to getting my way. No fruit was forbidden. Pulling some official notepaper from my attaché case, I penned a swift response, instructing Deveaux to establish the identity of Mademoiselle Courcel's intended husband as soon as possible and to prevent the union, no matter the method or cost. I sealed the envelope, marking it *Urgent*, and handed it to the attendant with the injunction that the letter be given personally to the stationmaster at the next stop for immediate transmission to the recipient in Paris. I gave him and the stationmaster a handsome tip.

Within the hour the train halted to take on water and coal. I watched the stationmaster take delivery of my letter. He looked in my direction and doffed his cap. The train began to move. No longer able to retrieve the letter, I started to realise the egregiousness of the act of betrayal I was committing – against my wife, Monique, and against Mademoiselle Courcel, whose life I was about to disrupt. Yet that thought was overshadowed by my determination to achieve my end –

to become a puppet master – whatever the cost to the lives of others. For me, the die was cast – and by my own hand.

The night seemed never-ending. I tried in vain to sleep. As I lay awake, I recalled a Greek sculpture I had seen of a young woman, exquisitely carved, lying on her side. It was one of the most sensuous creations in marble I had ever come across. For me, the figure's nude form – the sheer beauty of the breasts, the slender hips and the delicacy of the face – personified the body of Mademoiselle Courcel. I imagined lying beside her.

Whether I was asleep or still awake, I became aware of a dark shape entering my compartment. It stooped down beside my bed, its face without features I could recognise beyond a mirthless rictus smile. A voice whispered.

"So, Monsieur de Beaudreau, am I really to carry out the instruction in your letter? Is that really what you want – to interfere with the life of someone you have never met, only seen? I will proceed as you have indicated but I wish to be sure you understand the consequences that might unfold from your action. When the sun rises, it will be too late to rescind your order."

"Yes, it is what I want," I answered, also in a whisper. "Do exactly as I have instructed."

"So be it," the muffled voice replied. The shape extended an ice-cold hand. Unwillingly, I grasped it and shook it. "That is all I need to know," said the voice as the shape evaporated. I sank back on my pillow, sweating and short of breath, overwhelmed by a feeling of suffocation.

Eventually, the train emerged into daylight. Still recalling the apparition, I got up, checking that the compartment door was firmly locked from the inside. Was the shape I had seen a figment of my imagination or an actuality? The door was securely locked, the key beside the bed.

Before boarding the ship that would take me to the East, I spent two nights in Marseille in a comfortable hotel, reading reports of what awaited me in Cochinchina and sampling several bars. On the second evening, in one such bar down on the waterfront, a pretty young prostitute was offering her services. Without any hesitation or guilt I decided to accept, not because I found her beguiling but in order that I could imagine her body to be that of the girl in the skiff. In the end, we spent the entire night together in a small bedroom above the bar. In the morning, I paid her and the establishment's owner liberally. I returned to my hotel, bathed, packed and ate breakfast with no shame or regret for what I had done in the past hours. I was utterly unperturbed by my deplorable actions. I had become the victim of what I began to regard as a Faustian obsession. Perhaps Deveaux was the Devil.

After I had embarked, the purser handed me a telegram. Opening the envelope and unfolding the slip of paper inside, I was chilled by its contents.

> *The deed will be done. There is no going back. You will*
> *hear more on arrival at your destination.*
> *Deveaux*

I thought for a moment or two about how I should reply. Withdraw my instruction or simply acknowledge his message? There was only one shameless answer. I handed it to the purser, asking for it to be despatched before the ship was unmoored. It was brief.

> *Let the game begin.*
> *de B*

# CHAPTER TWO

Portraits of a Secret

I remember that summer well. Childhood behind me, I was able, at last, as an independent-minded young woman, to come and go as I pleased. Of course, my family emphasised the desirability of their only daughter marrying into a prestigious family and shortly after my eighteenth birthday I had been introduced to Alexandre de Mercier, an official in the presidential palace. We danced together several weeks later at a prestigious soirée in Paris, and over the following months we went to the theatre together to see plays by Racine and Molière. With his promising prospects at the presidential palace, my mother insisted Alexandre would make a fine husband, adding that he would bring social lustre to our family with its provincial origins.

Enjoying the freedom of womanhood, and not accountable to anyone, I was certainly in no hurry to be married. Moreover, Alexandre had not declared his feelings towards me and indeed had not once sought to kiss me, other than my gloved hand. Though I enjoyed his company, and he mine, and though I was acutely aware of how he turned the heads of other young women, we treated each other with a measurable degree of circumspection.

It was someone else that year who burst into my life to give me a depth of friendship I had never imagined possible: Célestine Vauquelin, my cousin, though my mother once disclosed in a moment of uncharacteristic indiscretion that she was illegitimate, not really "one of us".

For much of my childhood, Célestine, being nearly ten years older than me, was but a passing family acquaintance on her visits from Burgundy to our home in Normandy. Yet I recall vividly, even now, the impact she made – full of energy, noisy, constantly teasing and poking fun, laughing, forever testing everyone's patience. I always hid when she arrived, summoning the courage to be confronted by her. Becoming a painter of some repute, she moved, some years later, to live in Paris, just as my family had done. She rented a small atelier in Montmartre. After a few brief encounters, we began to see more of each other – window-shopping on the capital's fashionable streets, visiting museums and art galleries, meeting her friends in cafés. Vivacious, with a mane of red hair and her years' advantage, she was sparkling company. I enjoyed her *joie de vivre*, relished her gossip and learned from her strong opinions on the latest fads and fashions. I therefore did not hesitate to accept her invitation to stay with her that August in a friend's house in Provence.

It was my first visit to the south. The house, though small, was charming, set amongst trees but with a view over a river and the hills beyond. The weather was perfect too – warm sun-filled days, each seeming more pleasurable than the one before. And only three of us: just Célestine, me and an elderly housekeeper, Béatrice. In the first week, we went on walks, discussing Balzac, Stendhal and Prosper Mérimée, whose book had inspired Bizet's opera *Carmen*, which I was due to see with Alexandre in the autumn. Before the end of that first week, we had become the closest of confidantes, sharing intimate secrets with one another.

We continued our walks in the second week of my stay, with more discussion, more laughter, and often resting to read to each other and eat simple picnics which Béatrice prepared. One day, we walked along the river bank, holding hands, pausing to enjoy our picnic at the water's edge, beneath a weeping willow.

"Shall we swim?" asked Célestine.

"I cannot swim," I replied.

"That's not an obstacle. The water is shallow. You will come to no harm. Besides, I can teach you."

"But –"

"No excuses, Anne-Sophie. Undress! This is no time to be faint-hearted."

Célestine quickly removed her clothes. I fumbled, hesitant to do what she had done. She unbuttoned me, removed my dress and undid my corset, which she stuffed into her bag.

"You don't need that any more. Tonight, I will cut it up. Come on. Hurry!"

I quickly shed my chemise, stockings and shoes and followed her into the water. Frolicking naked in the cool silky water, being free from the constraint of a corset and overthrowing the conventional behaviour expected of a young woman in Parisian society gave me a physical pleasure I had not experienced before. Afterwards, we sat on the river bank, still unclothed, warmed by the sun filtering through the shade of the willow tree. Célestine described how women – clothed and unclothed – had been portrayed by artists through the ages. She, as an artist, wanted to paint women as they were, not stylised images.

"I hope, Anne-Sophie, you will let me paint you before we leave. You are so beautiful."

She leaned across and kissed me gently on the lips. My spine tingled, stirring feelings within me that again I was experiencing for the first time.

"Will you?" she asked, taking my hand in hers.

"Yes," I replied.

We dressed and walked arm in arm back to the house amongst the trees.

My remaining time in Provence gave me profound enjoyment. We went ever further on our walks, to the distant hills, enjoying picnics overlooking the valley below. The colours of the landscape were rich and dazzling – the broader, deeper sweeps of the hills and the valleys interspersed with the red-roof geometry of the villages. As we sought shade in the heat of the day, Célestine would take out her sketchbook and paintbox to capture the scene. One day I fell asleep in the warm sun. When I woke, Célestine showed me a sketch of a sleeping figure stretched out in the long grass, hat cast aside. It was inscribed *From Célestine to my beloved Anne-Sophie*. We heard the echo of a distant whistle, and saw, far away across the valley, a plume of smoke snaking from a train. An unwanted, painful reminder that the time was approaching for us to return to Paris. We sensed each other's sadness.

"Before we leave, I would like to paint you, as you promised I could," she said. "Not outside but at the house. I would like you to sit by the window overlooking the garden and valley below. That's where I wish to paint you."

"But of course," I replied. "Which dress do you wish me to wear – not that I have many to choose from?"

"I wish you to be unclothed."

I hesitated and blushed.

"It will be a painting for me to keep as a private, deeply personal reminder of our time together. No one else will ever see it."

I nodded assent.

The next day, Béatrice was dismissed early, so that I could sit for Célestine. Three days later, as evening approached, the small painting was finished. Célestine, excited, unveiled it. The style was almost impressionistic – to borrow, but approvingly, the new term – with bold, hurried brush strokes. She had portrayed me in profile, standing gazing out of the window, my hair loose about my shoulders, a breast discernible, one leg half tucked behind the other and a crumpled chemise at my feet. My other side was also visible, reflected indistinctly in a mirror on the background wall. I blushed when Célestine said I had an exquisite body, worthy of Venus.

"Thank you so much for allowing me to paint your portrait. Completing this canvas has given me immense satisfaction and confidence." She hugged me. "Tomorrow, our last day here, shall we go out on the river? I think it would be a fitting end to our month together, hidden away and freed from all constraint."

"I would like that," I replied. We held hands and kissed. As she prepared supper, I played a Beethoven sonata on the piano. I found it hard to hold back tears at our imminent return to Paris and convention.

*

That last afternoon on the river was perfect. Célestine refused to let me row, insisting that I read to her – some Baudelaire and Shakespeare's sonnets.

"Anne-Sophie, has Alexandre kissed you?" she asked, after I finished reading Sonnet 128. "Has he held you?"

"No, except to kiss my gloved hand. I'm not sure I would want him to do more."

"Why not?"

"I can't explain. I'm just not sure of him or of my feelings towards him. Besides, I'm uncertain how I ought to respond if he did seek to kiss me."

"I have kissed you," she said.

"That's different," I replied.

"Do you mind when I kiss you?"

"No. What you do is an expression of our deep friendship for one another."

"It is more than that, Anne-Sophie, so much more."

I struggled to find words to reply but none came.

"Anne-Sophie, you are so beautiful, so unblemished, so innocent. You accept human nature at face value, unlike a cynic such as I. With those attributes, perhaps you are a child descended from the gods."

"I am just me," I replied. "What more can I say?"

"I envy your poise, your allure. I'm amazed that Alexandre has been so neglectful, indeed so blind to your appeal. How could he resist the temptation to kiss you?"

I blushed at her compliment.

"Maman says that is how it should be. A man and a woman should not kiss before engagement."

Célestine rolled her eyes in horror.

"Have you ever been kissed by any man – on the lips? Has a man ever held you in tight embrace, his body pressed hard against yours?"

I shook my head.

"Anne-Sophie, later this year you will be nineteen but not yet passionately kissed. I can't believe it!"

I smiled, shrugging my shoulders. She laughed.

Turning back, we drifted, borne along by the current, Célestine merely stroking the surface of the water with her oars, while I cooled my fingers in the ripples they barely made, each of us lost in thought. Everything was still on the river bank. Preoccupied with the prospect of returning to Paris, I vaguely noticed a large, imposing eighteenth-century house with a long veranda. I would have ignored it completely were it not for a sudden puff of wind, a fluttering curtain and a movement in an open doorway, which caught my attention. A tall dark-haired man in an elegant white open-necked shirt stepped back from the doorway in which he had been standing. His features were indistinct. In a second he was gone. I turned back to Shakespeare to choose one last sonnet.

"Did you see him?" asked Célestine. "I think he may have waved at us."

"If he did, I didn't see," I replied.

"I wonder who he is, whose house it is? The architecture speaks of wealth, position and prestige."

"We are of no concern to people of his ilk," I said.

We drifted on. By the time we reached the jetty the sun had set behind the line of trees on the river bank. We slowly returned to the house, our secluded refuge in the woods, arm in arm, each reflecting on the days past and the times ahead. As we walked, our feet treading on the first of autumn's fallen leaves, the shadows of dusk closed around us. Summer was over, replaced by the chill of uncertainty.

As Béatrice prepared a simple supper, Célestine and I sat on our modest veranda, once more discussing books, though the tragic character of Carmen quickly altered the topic of conversation.

"I once seduced a young soldier," Célestine confided. "He was such a likeable young man but I soon tired of him, attracted, I must confess, by more beguiling lovers. He wrote to me later, recalling the time we had been intimate. The paper was smudged. Perhaps they were his tears."

"Célestine, don't be so cruel. Perhaps they were raindrops falling on some distant battlefield."

I sat amazed as she told me more of her life, of the men and women she had loved, of those she had despised, all in intimate detail.

"The truth, Anne-Sophie, is that I love beauty but even more than that I enjoy the pleasure of transgression – going beyond the boundary of decency, rejecting bourgeois morals, to do what I want to do. I was once like you – innocent. But it was not enough for me to be conventional. It was suffocating. I wanted to go further – to test myself and others, to see how far I and they could go." She looked at me, smiling. "I fear I may have corrupted you with my opinions, attitudes and behaviour while we've been together. You may think my confessions and conduct shocking. But whether I've appalled you or not, I want you to know that I have treasured your companionship these past weeks. I'm deeply sad we're parting tomorrow on our return to Paris. My heart is full of sorrow. I hope we will stay in touch. I say that in all sincerity, because I've fallen in love with you."

She took my hand and put it to her lips. I was lost for words. I didn't know how to express the tumult I felt.

"I'm sorry, Anne-Sophie. I have offended you. I should not have told you of my feelings towards you."

"Célestine, you have not offended me. Your profession of love has taken me aback, that's all. No one has said that to me before." I reached for her hand. "I am indeed innocent. I've so much to learn about life, about myself and about what it is to be a woman. You have been generous and honest in revealing details of your life, of yourself and of your attachments. I'm glad you did because you have given me a great deal to think about. What you've told me will remain locked within me, unshared with others. That is my promise. You have my trust. I hope I have yours."

"Thank you, Anne-Sophie. You do."

We sat in silence, looking at the distant river shrouded by dusk. She unpinned her hair, shaking it free. I could see how men – and women – had been attracted by its flame-red colour, by her figure-hugging dress, by her, just as I was. Yet I saw a touching vulnerability beneath the façade of bravura.

Béatrice called to say supper would be ready in thirty minutes. As we rose to change, Célestine asked if she could kiss me. Though Alexandre did not wish to do so, she did. I nodded. She pulled me close, wrapping her arms around my waist, and kissed my lips in a manner she had not done before – gently, sweetly. She had kissed me when we swam together in the river, when the portrait was unveiled, and on other occasions besides. But this kiss was deeper, more lasting, more expressive and more emotional.

We quickly changed and ate supper with a neighbour and his wife who had played their part in looking after us, and gossiped.

Shortly before midnight, after our guests and Béatrice had left, Célestine and I said goodnight. I could not sleep. I lay awake thinking of our weeks together – the literary discussions, the walks, the gossip, the joy of the river, of all that Célestine had revealed and the pleasure I had felt at my growing closeness to her. I would miss her greatly. Soon it would be my nineteenth birthday, bringing nearer the possibility that Alexandre might propose and the question of what I would reply. My mind would not rest. Such was the kaleidoscope of thoughts and feelings and the repetitive sound of the distant train whistle.

I heard a footstep. The bedroom door slowly opened. It was Célestine, her face framed by tumbling waves of hair and illuminated by a candle, her expression hesitant, questioning. She closed the door behind her. Approaching the bed, she put a finger to her lips. I pulled the covers back and gestured. Putting the candle down and shedding her nightdress, she slipped in beside me, undoing my nightgown and releasing the ribbon that held back my hair. Naked, we lay together. She stroked my skin, my hair, kissed me and held me tight. I had no urge to stop her. I wondered if being caressed by a man would be as enjoyable and comforting as the pleasure to which I had surrendered. Not letting go of me, she fell asleep. I was locked in her arms, whose grip I had no wish to loosen. When I woke in the morning, she was no longer beside me. The only trace of what had happened was my crumpled nightgown on the floor and my hair ribbon on the pillow.

During breakfast and afterwards, while we packed our few belongings, Célestine gave no sign of the intimacy of the night before.

Our journey back to Paris was long and tedious. Travelling third class on the train, there was no privacy. We sat beside each other, occasionally engaging in polite conversation but resisting the merest hint of physical contact, to avoid drawing unnecessary attention to ourselves. On the rack above, our baggage lay more intimately side by side, together with the leather tube containing her painting of me. On arrival at the Gare de Lyon, we quickly found a taxi to take me to my parents' apartment. As the coachman dismounted, we snatched one last kiss. I watched as the taxi and Célestine disappeared into the distance.

I was not to see her again for many weeks, though we frequently corresponded by letter, recalling in the blandest of terms – in case the contents were seen by others – our memories of Provence. Yet we knew the words we used carried, for us, a more special meaning. What had happened between us, particularly the night we shared a bed, had left an indelible mark upon me. She had stirred deep, dark emotions within me. I thought about Célestine often but could say nothing to others. Everything that had taken place had to remain a secret. For it to be otherwise was to risk scandal. I sought to resume life in Paris at home with my parents but, hard though I tried, I remained restless and distracted. My mother even asked if I felt unwell. I don't think she found my excuses convincing. Perhaps, she said, I was falling in love with Alexandre, or was worried that he had not observed my feelings towards him.

Late that autumn I accompanied Alexandre and his parents to a performance of *Carmen*. This being my first experience of opera, I was eager to see how the story of passionate love, jealousy and murder would unfold in music. The opera house was full, and Alexandre and his parents, being well known, acknowledged many friends and acquaintances as we made our way to the box. Once seated, I gazed in amazement at the elegance of the audience. I looked across to the boxes on the other side of the proscenium. Each one was full, their occupants, like me, brimming with excitement at the prospect of watching this highly controversial opera. The orchestra entered to wild applause and the audience hushed as the conductor raised his baton. I took one last look around the auditorium. Perhaps conjured by *Carmen*'s association with Célestine, our talks in Provence, I thought I saw in the box directly opposite the face of the man I had seen fleetingly at the house on the river. He was sitting next to an attractive well-dressed woman. He seemed to be looking at me, but I couldn't be sure. The lights dimmed, the overture began and I put him, and Célestine, out of my mind.

The opera was compelling, full of drama. I was transfixed. I chose to remain in the box during the first and second intervals, to reflect on what I had seen and heard, but before the last act Alexandre finally prevailed upon me to overcome my reluctance and join him with his Élysée Palace superior for champagne in the presidential box. As we navigated through the crowd, I looked for the man I thought I had glimpsed earlier but he was nowhere to be seen.

At the end of the opera, after prolonged applause, we made our way to the Place Boieldieu to find our carriage in the throng. At last it came. As I mounted the step and said goodbye to Alexandre's parents, I glanced along the pavement. There he was, the man I had seen in the box. He looked at me, smiled, bowed his head, but before I could acknowledge his gesture, Alexandre gently nudged me forward. I wasn't certain it was the man from the house by the river, who Célestine said had waved to us. If it were him, he was indeed handsome, with somewhat saturnine features, and he wore an elegant cloak.

A few days later Alexandre invited me to supper at one of Paris's most expensive restaurants. It was evident from the greeting he received that he had dined there before and had chosen it this time to impress me. We talked about many things, not least his future career, what he wanted to achieve and how much he enjoyed my company. It was a pleasant evening and at its conclusion, on arrival at my parents' apartment, he said goodnight and kissed me on the cheek, repeating how much he had enjoyed being with me and telling me of the compliments the gown I wore to the opera had received from his superior. I sensed that his kiss on my cheek and his flattering words might be a precursor of his intentions towards me.

About a fortnight afterwards, my father asked me to join him in the sitting room.

"Alexandre called on me two days ago to ask if I would object to him seeking your hand in marriage. He explained his prospects and the pleasure he takes in spending time with you. I said your mother and I would have no objection whatsoever. In fact, we would be delighted if he proposed. He said he will come tomorrow evening to do so. He does indeed have good prospects and your mother believes it's high time you were married, as do I. We assume you will accept. It will be a good match. What have you to say?"

I hesitated.

"I did not realise he believes he knows me well enough to ask to marry me. I thought I would have a little more time to myself before committing to marriage. At present, I have no particular feelings towards him."

"That will change, Anne-Sophie. He's handsome, a promising official and his family have money and a position in society – certainly more than us, I venture to say. And love is not instant. It grows."

"I will consider what he has to say. That is all I can promise."

"So be it. But don't let this opportunity slip through your fingers. Your mother and I expect you to accept."

That night I was in turmoil. What should I do? If only I could speak to Célestine, but she was not in Paris, her precise whereabouts unknown to me. Where did my loyalty lie – to my parents, to do as they expected, or to Célestine, with her different view of life, or to Alexandre? Or to myself? Should I do what I wanted?

The following evening, as he had advised, Alexandre came to the apartment. My mother had persuaded me to wear the off-the-shoulder gown I wore to the opera, urging me, as I dressed, to accept his proposal. Left alone with him, but conscious my mother was eavesdropping, I dutifully listened to Alexandre's overtures of marriage. Despite grave misgivings, I felt obliged to say yes. He kissed me – his lips on mine – but his embrace did not give me that frisson of pleasure and excitement I had experienced when Célestine kissed me. That night I went to bed in even greater emotional turmoil.

I wrote to Célestine the next day to tell her what had happened, berating her for not being available to advise me what to do. There was no reply. A week later, she wrote to apologise profoundly for her silence. She had been in Spain, she explained, painting, continually moving from place to place and so unable to leave a forwarding address. She regretted that I had been placed in an impossible position. Her sorrow at my decision was acute. If it was my firm intention to marry Alexandre, she dearly hoped that she and I would remain close friends. She added that whatever might happen to our friendship after my marriage, her portrait of me would provide a lasting reminder of our love for one another. I replied immediately, saying that she and I should meet, but Célestine's response declared that would not be possible. She would find our conversation unbearable.

The weeks that followed were a time of oppressive sadness for me – the prospect of becoming Alexandre's wife, of losing my freedom, of his impending sexual possession of me and the reality of my lack of love for him. My despair was all the heavier because of the bond, both physical and emotional, I had forged with Célestine in Provence. Had I been right to succumb to her? Was my despair an expression of guilt at what she and I had done? Should I go to Confession and seek forgiveness? I tried once more to persuade her to meet but again she refused, leaving me with no one to whom I could turn. The occasions I spent with Alexandre bordered on the mechanical and I struggled to conceal my lack of interest in the preparations for my wedding. And yet another fact troubled me: when I left the apartment, I often sensed that I was being followed. I saw no one, neither did my mother, to whom I spoke about it. She put it down to pre-marriage nerves. That did not reassure me. I felt a growing malevolence surrounding me.

At Easter the following year I joined my parents in Trouville, the last time we would be together before my marriage to Alexandre. One afternoon, I walked with my mother along the beach, listening to her repeated assurances that all would be well. But her words were unconvincing and did little to put my mind at rest. I had a deep sense of foreboding. Oblivious to everything around me, all I could think of was Célestine.

Autumn and the arrangements for my marriage were well advanced when at short notice Alexandre asked to see me.

"Dearest Anne-Sophie, I'm afraid it is no longer possible for us to be married. Certain circumstances have arisen that make our union

impossible. I know you will be disappointed and that I will be much diminished in your estimation but there is no other course of action. Better a little unhappiness now than a lifetime of misery to come. Please forgive me."

"What are these circumstances that have arisen?" I asked, scarcely able to hide my relief.

"I cannot say," he replied.

"I see. In the absence of an explanation, I can only assume that your earlier expressions of affection and loyalty were premature, that your thoughts and feelings have turned elsewhere. I will inform my father of your decision. He and my mother will be sorely disappointed and will likely seek a better explanation than the one you have given me. But I accept your decision and, in the circumstances, I consider it appropriate. Perhaps for me it will prove a lucky escape."

"A lucky escape for both of us," he added. "I will write to your father immediately."

With those words, he attempted to kiss my hand but I denied him the gesture.

My parents were mortified when I told them. They asked whether there was anything I might have done to cause him to terminate the engagement. I immediately thought of what Célestine and I had done. Perhaps she had revealed our secret to a friend and its disclosure had found its way into Paris gossip, with inevitable consequences.

"I do not know, Maman, what has caused this volte-face. Perhaps his letter to Papa will reveal more."

Alexandre's letter arrived the next day but shed no further light on the reason for his decision. My father intended to reply at once, demanding further information and threatening legal redress for the embarrassment the situation would cause and compensation for the expenditure the preparations had already incurred. I made him promise not to do so, since such a step might result in actions both sides would regret and inflame the inevitable gossip. It was better to let the matter rest and for us to say to our friends and acquaintances that the engagement had ended by mutual agreement on the grounds of incompatibility.

I lost no time in writing to Célestine. We agreed to meet at the

Louvre, amid the crowds and bustle of which we would be inconspicuous.

"Célestine, did you reveal to anyone what happened in Provence – a careless word, a slip of the tongue? I would forgive you if you had. I just need to know whether that is Alexandre's reason. Or could it have been Béatrice? After all, she saw how close we became."

"My own Anne-Sophie, I promised never to disclose our secret. I have not told anyone and my painting of you remains under lock and key. And it could not have been Béatrice. She died several months ago, more advanced in years and less robust of health than she led us to believe. I have no idea what might have prompted Alexandre to reject you in this cruel way. But, though it may be painful and the gossip hurtful, you are now once again free. I suggest we go away for a while, until the tittle-tattlers have found a new subject to chatter about."

"I would like that, but we must be careful," I replied.

A day or so later Célestine wrote to say she had been commissioned to paint a landscape for a client near Honfleur. She would be there for some two weeks, in a house she would have to herself, and suggested that I come to spend a long weekend. I replied quickly to accept.

The house, near the seashore, was basic but secure. A few fishermen's cottages were less than a kilometre away.

On our first afternoon, we walked on the beach and then sat talking in front of the fire late into the evening. Shortly before midnight, contentedly weary, I admitted I was ready for sleep.

"I've prepared a bedroom for you."

"Célestine, I would like us to be together. I've missed you being close to me."

She took my hand and smiled. "I would like that too."

We went upstairs.

"I would like you to undress me."

"Of course," she replied.

It was as though we had never parted. To have her hold, caress and kiss me stirred an aching longing within me. We fell asleep, as in Provence, with me tightly locked in her strong arms.

The remainder of the weekend was a time of profound joy. While Célestine painted, I prepared meals and walked along the beach. On the last afternoon, I was sitting on the sand reading. A shadow approached me. It belonged to an elderly man, roughly dressed but well spoken. He doffed his hat.

"I haven't seen you in these parts before, mademoiselle. Visiting?"

"Yes. Visiting my friend. She's over there, painting. That's her profession. She's an artist."

He turned to look in the direction I indicated. I thought he would walk on, but he addressed me again.

"You're an attractive young woman. Not married yet?"

"No, not married yet," I replied. "Perhaps it will happen someday."

"Where do you live?"

"Paris," I said, beginning to find his unabashed curiosity somewhat intrusive.

"It is years since I've been there – too big, too smoky for me. I enjoy being here. But I still like reading about it – all that scandal, all that crime."

"I think you're being rather hard on the city," I replied.

"Perhaps I am. Well, I must be on my way. But before I take my leave, I have in my pocket a Paris newspaper. I've finished with it – it's a couple of days old. Would you like it?"

"Yes, please."

"Here, it's yours."

With that, he raised his hat and walked on, turning after a few steps to call out: "You're a real beauty. If only I were younger . . . But I'm sure others have their eyes on you." He waved. I reciprocated.

That evening, Célestine and I sat in front of the fire. I thumbed through the newspaper. There was little of interest other than a report of some burglaries.

"Hmm, that's not far from my studio," remarked Célestine.

We went to bed. Once more, I felt safe, protected and loved, and – for the first time – experienced intense physical pleasure.

*

I returned to Paris alone, determined to create a new life for myself. A few days later, Célestine sent me a handwritten message asking to meet urgently that evening, at a café. She was visibly discomposed.

"The painting – the one of you – has been taken from my studio. Nothing else was stolen, just your portrait."

"I thought you said it was secure."

"It was – that is, I thought it was. I had concealed it, still in its leather tube, well out of sight and beyond the risk of accidental discovery. Some of the canvases propped against the wall had been disturbed but nothing else was moved, damaged or taken. The only evidence of theft was the forced lock on the studio door. Whoever broke in appeared to know what they were looking for. I'm so sorry, Anne-Sophie."

"Are you sure it's the only thing that was taken?"

"Yes, I've checked a dozen times. But the person who took the portrait left this note."

She passed me a small sheet of innocuous-looking paper – the kind used for personal correspondence – with bold black ink handwriting on it. I read the chilling words.

You cannot possess what belongs to someone else.

"What does it mean?" I asked.

"I don't know."

"Have you informed the police?"

"Yes. They were already in the neighbourhood making enquiries following the recent burglaries. I said that someone had forcibly entered the studio but it appeared nothing had been stolen."

"Did you tell them about the note? Show it to them?"

"I didn't."

"But they might have been able to trace the handwriting."

She looked down, her hands clasped.

"There's something I did not tell you. On the back of the painting, I wrote a dedication: 'To my dearest and beautiful lover Anne-Sophie'."

I swallowed hard.

"For that reason, I could not tell them. They would have become aware of my inclinations – and of us." She took my hand, her eyes moist with tears. "I'm so sorry."

"Célestine, please, no remorse. Things are as they are. At least we now know there is no connection between Alexandre's termination of the engagement and my portrait, since his decision preceded the theft. Yet I am concerned someone must have known about the painting and where you had put it. Perhaps it was someone in Provence, or on the train. Are you sure it was not Béatrice?"

"I'm certain it was not her. I was so careful to conceal what I was doing. Anne-Sophie, I am so sorry," she said again.

"Célestine, I should like us to go away – and not just for a weekend. I would like it to be for longer so we can be together again, as we were in Provence. Why don't we travel to Spain? You can paint there and I know I'll be able to find something to do."

"But I have little money. How will we survive?"

"My late aunt left me a small inheritance. It's only a small amount but it will enable us to live independently for a while."

Over the next few weeks, meeting whenever we could and trying – not always successfully – to refrain from any public display of affection, we secretly hatched our plan, on scraps of paper which we later burned, as we imagined spies would do. Once everything was ready I broke the news to my parents, explaining that some months in Spain was the best way to recover from Alexandre's rejection, which was still the subject of tittle-tattle in the newspapers and gossip at soirées: a dull provincial family had received their social comeuppance. After several fruitless efforts to dissuade me, they reluctantly agreed and helped make the necessary financial arrangements – even contributing a generous sum to supplement the inheritance. A week later, Célestine and I left Paris for Madrid and, after a short stay in the city, we arrived in Seville, where we rented a room in a house occupied by other young artists.

Shortly afterwards, a handwritten note was delivered, addressed to Célestine.

You cannot possess what belongs to someone else.

We chose to ignore it, finding even greater comfort in our love for one another yet nonetheless concerned that we were being observed, pursued. The note reminded me of the sense I'd had in Paris that I was being watched, which I decided not to mention to Célestine. We behaved with caution and vigilance, making concerted efforts to join in the communal activities of the house but occasionally doing separate things during the day. Sometimes I would walk with Sancha, a vivacious flamenco dancer several years older than me. She would often dance for us on the veranda in the evening. With long black hair, vivid green eyes and a lithe body, she was for me the epitome of the doomed Carmen. The guitar player, and Sancha's lover, was Francisco, a talented artist whose paintings were as wild as his music. He fascinated Célestine, who sketched him several times, as did he her. He asked if he could paint my portrait also. She urged me to agree.

I sat for him, wearing, at his instigation, one of Sancha's flamenco costumes and with my hair pinned up. Célestine adored the finished painting, which portrayed me with a resolute expression, the yellow dress striking against its background of a white curtain and an open window. Not to be outdone, she asked me to pose once more for her. While Francisco praised her skill, he said he would do even better next time. To ensure harmony, I agreed to sit for both of them. Eager to compete with Célestine, Francisco proposed that they paint me in the style of Velazquez's *Venus at her Mirror*. After considerable debate and somewhat nervously, I agreed to pose unclothed – lying on my stomach on a bed covered by a pink counterpane, my face turned away, reading a book. Upon completion, Francisco's painting was considered by general acclamation, including Célestine's, to have triumphed. His light, silky touch but strong composition – a shaft of sunlight between half-drawn curtains, a glimpse of my breast, the exaggerated line of my waist and the contours of my back and buttocks – were simple yet arresting. With no facial profile my identity had been cleverly concealed. Célestine willingly conceded defeat. She dearly wanted to hang his canvas in our bedroom, but

Francisco insisted that it be placed in the dining-room, on the wall opposite his impressive portrayal of Sancha in a deep-red flamenco dress whose neckline traced the valley of her breastbone almost down to her waist. We came to call it *The Mujer* – the woman.

The weeks passed. For me and for Célestine it was a time of idyllic, sensual bliss – carefree days bathed in sunlight, the emotional intensity of guitar music in the evening and a shared bed of secrets at night. Defying convention gave me a shiver of excitement. Paris seemed so remote. But we knew it could not last. Once our money ran out, we would have to return to society and its suffocating strictures.

CHAPTER THREE

The Love of Money

I recall vividly the day I was dismissed. A long-serving and diligent police officer, I was wrongly blamed – at least, that was my opinion – for a miscarriage of justice that had had unfortunate consequences. There is no need to disclose the details but yes, I had made, as we all do from time to time, a mistake – a serious mistake, even – committed an uncharacteristic error of judgement. I had acknowledged it and sought to make amends. The commissioner of police, a pompous individual ever seeking greater professional glory, preferred to sacrifice me rather than his deputy, who bore considerable culpability for the way the case had been handled. The ignominy of dismissal and the unexpected, untimely loss of income lit within me an inextinguishable fire of revenge.

With a frail wife and still obliged to earn a living, I became a private investigator, prepared to use my skills to financial advantage. Repaying my kindness to her late husband, the widow of a former colleague provided a couple of rooms in a second-floor apartment near Notre-Dame cathedral. I was proud when my name was put on the door the day I began. The formidable concierge, Madame Mallet, was ready to pass my name amongst her contacts and quickly proved an invaluable source of gossip, a key vein of information for anyone in my trade. I soon had my first cases – nothing out of the ordinary – resulting in some modest remuneration.

Before long I decided to increase my income and that the best way to do this would be to respond to calls for assistance from those whose greed I could exploit for my own financial gain. I therefore became less interested in helping the oppressed, in putting right the miscarriages of justice others had suffered, ideals that had informed my initial caseload. Instead, I sought clients I could turn to my advantage – not just by siphoning more money from them but by using them to strike back at discredited social and judicial systems. This was not a difficult objective for me to pursue. I had long despised the rich for their wealth, their arrogance, their pride and the misuse of their vast personal patronage. And during my extensive police career, I had observed unparalleled corruption in high places, no more so than under Louis Napoleon's empire. I had witnessed first-hand the extent to which malefactors easily bought their way out of trouble, drawing on their wealth to do so. Now I had the chance to make such people serve my turn, capitalising on my experience and informants to blackmail them. My first clients in this category soon showed that with patience and application it was a rich seam to mine. Then came a client with much greater promise.

Émile de Beaudreau came to see me one afternoon. I remember that day well. Assured, chest full of pride, well-dressed and sleek in appearance, he sought my help in a most extraordinary commission. He had seen a young woman at the opera. Though he had caught a glimpse of her once before, he did not know her. He was keen to find out her name.

"May I ask why?"

He paused for a moment, clearly trying to conjure a plausible reason.

"I wish to make her acquaintance," he replied.

"For what purpose?" I asked.

He again looked thoughtful.

"It's a confidential matter, Monsieur Deveaux, to do with my work at the Ministry."

"I see," I replied, in a manner that clearly conveyed I was unconvinced by his answer. "Monsieur de Beaudreau, if I were to undertake this task I would prefer to know the real reason."

"I wish to make her acquaintance," he repeated. "I glimpsed her some time ago in a skiff on a river in Provence. She was with someone else – another woman. I saw her again more recently, at the opera, on this occasion with a male companion and an older couple. She is an attractive young woman and since we were near neighbours in Provence – my family own a house there – I would like to have the pleasure of meeting her."

His answer still seemed unconvincing, incomplete, and I think he knew that to be the case. From my long police career, I know when people are lying. He had just uttered an untruth. Judging him across the table, I was certain he wanted to meet the young woman for a less neighbourly purpose. If that were the case, and I provided what he wanted, it would come at a price.

"Why would you wish to do that, monsieur? After all, if what I have heard is correct, you are already committed to another."

"It's a whim, Monsieur Deveaux, just a whim. I'm sure you have whims."

"I have never heard of such a request before, but if you wish me to establish the identity of this young woman I will see what I can do – provided you are prepared to pay my fee. And it may take time. I have other cases to see to."

"Payment of your fee is not a problem. Do whatever is necessary to find out who she is as quickly as you can and report to me accordingly."

"If I succeed, do you wish me to approach her?"

"On no account should you do so. Once I know her name, I will decide what to do next. Please contact me at this address. While I appreciate you may have other clients, I insist you proceed promptly as I will shortly be leaving Paris and I need to meet the young woman before my departure. Is that understood? I will make it worth your while."

"Yes," I replied. "Can you describe her?"

He pulled several sketches from a leather attaché case. Each was different and his own verbal description was equally unhelpful. All he could give me was the date of the opera performance and the approximate position of the box in which she had been sitting. I thanked him for his commission and promised to do what I could.

"Only you and I must know about this, Monsieur Deveaux, absolutely no one else. Complete confidentiality, do you understand?"

I nodded.

He rose to leave. He appeared nervous, no doubt because he had disclosed to me a personal matter he would have preferred to keep concealed. He had shared a secret. He drew fifty francs from his pocket and placed the sum on my desk.

"I hope that is enough to cover your immediate fee and expenses. If you need more, please let me know at once."

With that, he left.

I started making enquiries, but not about the young woman, about de Beaudreau. He came, as Madame Mallet had intimated, from a rich family steeped in the law but, she said, accompanied by the smell of corrupt practice. He was a senior official in the Foreign Ministry, apparently soon to be posted, and it seemed that what I had heard was correct: he was soon to marry Monique d'Aurevalle, daughter of a rich industrialist who moved in the high social circles of Paris. Why should he want to find out the identity of a young woman he did not know in order to meet her? I asked some of my old contacts about him and his family. Initially, not much emerged that I hadn't found out already, but later I learned that, like his father, de Beaudreau was a womaniser, known to enjoy the company of beautiful women attracted to him by his money rather than his looks or character. According to the concierge, some of them were prostitutes.

If this information was even partially correct, it suggested that the man who had sought my help probably had it in mind to bed the young woman before his marriage – to exercise some warped form of droit de seigneur. Should I protect her from this predator by telling him that, despite my diligent enquiries, it had been impossible to find her? Or should I cast aside concern for her well-being in favour of my own selfish financial interest by giving him the information he required and seeing what else he might ask me to do? After some reflection, and stifling my scruples, I decided to do what de Beaudreau had asked, in the hope that it might lead to more income for me at a time when my wife was becoming frailer.

It did not take long to establish the young woman's identity – Anne-Sophie Courcel – or indeed the identity of those with her in the box at the Opéra Comique. My enquiries revealed that the young man with her that evening was Monsieur Alexandre de Mercier, an official at the presidential palace and, according to rumour, likely to be her husband. I decided not to disclose this information to my client immediately but to make him wait, in order to judge, from the persistence of his reminders to me to hurry up, the extent and urgency of his determination to seduce Mademoiselle Courcel. Just how far would de Beaudreau go before he was married? And would his determination be such as to provide me with the opportunity to squeeze more money from him? He pressed me again and again for the result of my enquiries and each time I counselled him to be patient.

I resolved to strike on the eve of his departure for Cochinchina. I sent him an urgent letter via the Foreign Ministry divulging Mademoiselle Courcel's name but not the identity of the young man it was likely she would marry. I half expected to receive a reply stating that he no longer wished to pursue the matter. To my pleasant surprise he replied in an urgent letter sent en route to Marseille instructing me not only to establish the identity of her intended husband but also to do whatever was necessary to block the marriage.

That surprise, and relief at the prospect of further income, rapidly gave way to rage. It was another repugnant example of the self-serving use of wealth and influence to achieve personal gratification at the expense of someone else's happiness. Did I really wish to carry out such an odious instruction, which went against all my previous professional and moral instincts? I looked down onto the street below, debating whether I should simply ignore what he wanted me to do – let his letter go unanswered – and close the file, or reply, telling him that I could not accede to what he had instructed and that he should find someone else to do his bidding. Or should I comply with his instruction and proceed to destroy the life and happiness of Mademoiselle Courcel? If I took the latter course, however unjust it may be, I would earn more money and might well have the chance to blackmail him later and, through the proceeds, finally afford for my ailing wife and I to leave the cold and grime of Paris for the warmth of the south. It was a case of principles versus personal interest, following my conscience or putting it aside. Ultimately, lured by money and the comforts it could bring, I succumbed to temptation and chose to be destructive. The deed would be done. The mademoiselle might suffer temporary unhappiness but he would be lastingly ensnared in the viper's nest. I replied to de Beaudreau accordingly and, after the despatch of my message, I considered how I would achieve the termination of the intended marriage of Alexandre de Mercier and Anne-Sophie Courcel.

In any investigation observation is an essential component. A viper is silent and vigilant, patiently seeking out its prey and, when sighted, considering the best moment to strike. I had learned this as a police officer and such tactics were as relevant now as they had been in the past. I therefore began to observe my two victims.

Alexandre de Mercier was a tall young man, well-dressed, articulate and, by all accounts, ambitious. His family, who were from Paris, were relatively wealthy, well-connected and generally respected. He had a younger brother, an officer in the army, and an older sister, who was married to a highly promising lawyer. Of the three siblings, it was Alexandre who had the best prospects by virtue of his post at the presidential palace. He had already received two earlier-than-usual promotions, and marriage would no doubt improve his prospects at the palace even further. I had the opportunity one day to get close enough to hear him speak. He had a polished accent but he seemed rather dull, possibly lacking a sense of humour. My other observation was that he was prone to snobbery, not unexpected in the social circles in which he mingled.

Mademoiselle Courcel, whom I was frequently able to observe, was indeed young and beautiful as de Beaudreau had described her. She was tall, slim and stylishly but not extravagantly dressed, as one would expect of a provincial family who had left Normandy for Paris. In the city's social hierarchy, she and her family were bourgeois rather than haute bourgeois. As a result, their expenditure was limited compared to that of the de Mercier family. Her older brother, an army officer, had been killed at Sedan in the Franco-Prussian war of 1870. The family had a modest number of friends in the city. The mademoiselle often walked the streets alone, when not with her mother. Occasionally she would spend time with her feisty cousin, Célestine Vauquelin, an artist from a long-established family in Burgundy, who had come to Paris to paint. They would stroll together, gazing in shop windows, and chat over coffee.

It was hard to find a plausible reason to end the engagement. Eventually, I decided that the Courcel family would have to be the cause of the rupture. I wrote to Alexandre de Mercier, "out of courtesy and respect", I claimed, to say that I had read of his engagement to Mademoiselle Courcel and, in the circumstances, felt obliged to draw to his attention some unsolicited information I had received from a well-wisher of his, who wished to remain anonymous. According to what I had been told, his fiancée's family had recently become indebted following the loss of savings in a speculative venture embarked upon in the hope of increasing their income. The venture had failed and as a consequence the family were considering leaving Paris as discreetly as possible to return to Normandy, where they would be better able to live a more frugal lifestyle and thus slowly repay their creditors. It was for him to decide, my letter concluded, whether to accept this unsolicited information at its face value or to commence enquiries into its veracity. If the latter, I was ready to act on his behalf.

De Mercier asked to meet me. I repeated what I had written, adding that in view of his career he might think it best to reconsider his proposal of marriage – assuming, of course, that the information I had provided was true. I forbade him to disclose that I was the source of the information he had received, since I in turn had received it from a source who did not want their anonymity to be compromised. Snob that he was, de Mercier swallowed the story I had spun and later wrote to me to say that he had ended the engagement and wished to thank me for ensuring the good name of his family and the preservation of his career. With his letter came a small gratuity.

My guilt at what I had done to the name and reputation of the Courcel family did not last long. My note to de Beaudreau informing him that the engagement had been terminated earned me a further substantial payment. There I thought the matter would end. But following his payment came a further explicit instruction that I should continue to observe the mademoiselle and report to him regularly, providing details of her activities. He also requested that I send him an image of her, perhaps a photograph, which he could keep in his private possession. In due course, he would return to Paris on leave and seek to make contact with her. I replied that I would do my best, given the demands of other cases, and asked him to deposit a further amount, which he did. I added that providing a photograph of the young woman would be hard to achieve as I could not foresee any circumstances in which I could request her to go to a studio for a picture to be taken.

It was becoming increasingly evident to me that de Beaudreau was consumed by a powerful obsession, one that carried many risks for him. While there might also be some danger for me in feeding it, I put the possibility aside as I contemplated the further sums of money I would earn from my vicarious voyeurism. He would come to realise that he was in my ever-tightening, ineluctable grip. The more he wanted the more I would know and the more I knew the more he would have to pay. I had become the joker in a pack of cards.

One day, with little to do, I had the time to follow Mademoiselle Courcel once more. On this occasion, I was able to observe her at the Louvre in the company of her cousin Célestine, whom I had seen before. They clearly enjoyed each other's company, giggling and whispering as they admired portraits of women. Leaving the gallery, they walked arm in arm – conduct I had not previously noted – through the Tuileries garden. When they parted I saw them surreptitiously kiss each other on the cheek. To a casual passer-by it may have appeared a perfunctory gesture but to me – a keen scrutiniser, over the years, of human behaviour – it indicated a greater meaning. The kiss, accompanied by a lingering close embrace, denoted a deeper import. I decided spontaneously, without consulting my client, to establish precisely what that import might be. In doing so, I took a further step towards compromising my own morals – a step, in hindsight, I should not have taken. No longer thinking dispassionately about my motives and principles, I was becoming driven solely by the acquisition of money, behaving like those whom I despised so much. Blinded by greed, it did not occur to me in the slightest that I was accelerating a train of events that would have tragic consequences.

With de Mercier's engagement at an end and my client now ensconced in the office of the administrator of Cochinchina in Hue, I made a journey south to Provence to begin the search for a place for my wife and I to live and, moreover, to see the location where de Beaudreau claimed he first glimpsed Anne-Sophie Courcel.

It did not take long to find the de Beaudreau summer residence, perhaps better described as a summer palace. It was large, impressive, a bold statement of unquantifiable wealth and, in my opinion, extremely vulgar. I stood on the river bank beneath the veranda to judge the point at which he might have seen the boat. I then walked further along, asking a few local people whether they had noticed two young women on the water the previous summer. I had little luck until near the end of the day, when in a bar I got talking to an elderly boatman who recalled two young women who had hired a skiff from him for an afternoon on the river.

"I remember them well. The older of the two – a brazen one, if you ask me – was good at rowing and at banter with me. The other one was younger, quietly spoken and a real beauty."

"Do you know where they were staying?"

"I don't know for sure, but on the hill above the river over there you'll find a few secluded houses. I think the older woman said they were in one of those – she described it as their house in the trees. There used to be a gentle old soul – Béatrice was her name – who looked after one particular house. It may have been that one, but she died some time ago. Her daughter, Claudette, may remember. Why do you want to know?"

"An acquaintance of mine has asked, since I was in these parts on other business, to find out what happened to them."

I bought him another Calvados to deflect him from asking more questions.

The next day, following the boatman's directions, I found Claudette, tending her mother's grave in the local cemetery. We chatted about the weather and where I might look for a house that my wife and I could rent to escape Paris.

"Depends how much you can afford. There are some grand houses around here but a few more modest ones too."

"My wife and I would like a small house, safe but out of the way, with a view of the river."

She paused. "My late mother, God rest her soul, used to work in a small house near a few others high up on the hill amongst some trees. I went there once. You could see the river in the distance. My mother enjoyed working there – she liked the owner, and was always fascinated by the friends she allowed to borrow it. Last year, not long before she died, she looked after two young women who came to stay for the month of August. She said they would go out for long walks and never stopped talking. One, the older of the two, was an artist. Just before they left, my mother happened to catch a glimpse of a painting she had done of the younger girl – naked. My mother, like me not one for that sort of thing, nevertheless said it was a beautiful picture. On their last day, the older girl put the canvas in a leather carrying tube. According to my mother, she held it tightly as though she was terrified of losing it."

I thanked Claudette and, after a few more minutes of idle chat, I left, satisfied I had heard enough about a painting which, if I could find it, might earn me more money from my client. At last, he would possess an image of her.

Not long after my return to Paris, I once again observed the two young women, first window-shopping, and then at a café. Afterwards, I followed Célestine Vauquelin to what appeared to be her atelier in the rue Frochot in the notorious Pigalle district. I asked my concierge to find out on which floor she lived. The answer was swift: her studio was on the top floor. I had to find a means of entering the atelier when she was not there. A few days later the opportunity arose, coinciding with a spate of night-time robberies in the neighbourhood – petty theft, you might call it, and not surprising in such a risqué area.

I observed the two women one afternoon saying farewell at the Gare Saint-Lazare; according to the clerk, they had bought tickets to Honfleur. After buying one for myself, I watched Mademoiselle Vauquelin board a train, with Mademoiselle Courcel promising to join her shortly. That evening, an old police informer told me over a drink in a bar that the local *gardiens* were finding it hard to stop the robberies in Pigalle. Though the pickings were often meagre, there was still enough value in the stolen items for the thieves to make their criminal ends meet. That didn't worry me. The burglaries would be good cover for what I intended to do.

After a drink in another bar, I judged it was time to become a temporary thief. Mingling with hawkers and prostitutes amidst the shadows, I approached number 5 rue Frochot. The concierge was not in her cubicle by the entrance. I tiptoed along the hall and saw she was asleep in the back room, an empty wine glass on the table in front of her. I quickly went up to the top floor and with ease forced the lock. Lighting a candle – part of the kit I always carried in my pockets – I quickly inspected the studio. It was small, with a truckle bed in one corner, a wardrobe, a washstand and items a young woman requires for her toilet. On the other side of the room were some paintings propped against the wall, a table strewn with paraphernalia – paints, inks, pens, brushes and scraps of cloth – and an easel. I rifled through the paintings but saw none of a naked young woman looking like Mademoiselle Courcel. Then I remembered what Claudette had said: the picture had been put in a carrying tube. I heard footsteps below and began to sweat. I had to hurry. Where would the artist hide a precious picture? I searched the wardrobe. Nothing. There was only one place left – under the bed. I got down on my hands and knees and rummaged. I discovered an assortment of bits and pieces and a small battered rattan suitcase, then right at the back against the wall I felt something cylindrical. I pulled out a long leather canister. I opened the top – another lock easily prised – and pulled out a rolled canvas. Half unscrolling it, I saw in the flickering candlelight that it was a painting of a young woman. Hearing more footsteps in the stairwell, I quickly put the canvas back. I had one last mischievous thought – to leave an anonymous note. In hindsight, I cannot think what made me do it. I had in my coat pocket a package of notepaper my wife had asked me to buy for her. I removed a sheet and, compounding the mischief, used one of Mademoiselle Vauquelin's pens and bottles of ink to write:

You cannot possess what belongs to someone else.

Leaving the note on the table, I slipped out of the studio and crept downstairs. The concierge was still asleep in the back room as I left the building.

Early the next morning, I examined the painting. It was an excellent likeness, well executed and understatedly but undeniably erotic. The inscription on the back confirmed my suspicion: the two women were lovers. Yet that was not my concern. What was paramount was despatching the portrait to de Beaudreau and making him pay a good price for it. Then my dealings with him would be over – that is, unless and until my finances required otherwise – and I could begin to make arrangements for my wife and I to go to Provence and live in the house amongst the trees. I went to the post office and sent a telegram:

In accordance with your instructions, excellent image ready for despatch following receipt of 500 francs.

The next day I received a reply:

Send image soonest to agreed address. Collect sum from Banque de l'Indochine in 3 days in your name.

*

It was soon time to go to Honfleur to play a game. Aware that Mademoiselle Courcel had already left to join her cousin, I travelled there too. In so small a village, it was not difficult, by asking a few questions and through observation, to learn the whereabouts of the two women. Thus, with a Paris newspaper protruding from my pocket, I was at last able to come face to face with the young beauty about whom my client was so obsessed and alert her to the thefts in Paris under cover of which I had managed to steal a most precious personal item. As I walked away along the beach, I was acutely aware I had intruded upon her and Mademoiselle Vauquelin's private lives in a recklessly despicable way, all to satisfy the sexual fantasy of the fixated Émile de Beaudreau. For my part, I had been driven by money, with the result that I had behaved like the very people I loathed. I told myself I had to regard it as business. And with the despatch of the painting it would be over. My wife and I could leave for Provence. Then my conscience could begin to clear. What I had done would be in the past, forgotten.

But money can be as unshakable an obsession as a beautiful young woman. When I learned that the mademoiselles were travelling to Spain, I resolved to follow them, the opportunity to demand more funds from de Beaudreau being too good to miss. And to my horror the matter did not end there. He imposed a further assignment upon me. For a while, he had been at my mercy because of the secret he had shared. I could easily blackmail him if I so wished. To that extent he had become my slave. But following the arrival of the portrait he knew that I had committed an illegal act, irrespective of the fact that he had inspired me to the theft. Now I was equally enslaved to him. Becoming apprehensive about the possible consequences of my actions I sought to persuade him to seek assistance from someone else. De Beaudreau would not have it, insisting I lay the ground for the possible annulment of his marriage to Monique d'Aurevalle, on the basis of whatever pretexts I could manufacture. If I did not do as he asked, he would create trouble for me – he appeared to ignore the fact that I could do the same for him. We were locked together.

Nightmare

CHAPTER FOUR

Orientation

It was a pleasant, unremarkable but tediously long voyage to Saigon. There was little to do on board other than to read and to make polite conversation. As the vessel neared its destination and the start of a new phase in my life – as the wife of the deputy to the French Resident Superior in the imperial city of Hue – I took stock.

My departure from Paris heralded multiple absences – of soirées, opulence, being envied for capturing Émile and, of course, of city gossip, which I had always relished. Not long before leaving the capital, I attended a grand ball, wearing a sumptuous silk gown which I subsequently decided to take with me to my new abode. My escort that night, I recall, was Alexandre de Mercier, a rather solemn young man whose engagement to Mademoiselle Anne-Sophie Courcel – of whom I knew nothing other than what he told me – had ended because of her family's apparent financial difficulties. A pen-and-ink sketch of me that evening, seated, surrounded by a bevy of ladies who appeared to be engrossed by every word I uttered, had even appeared in the magazine *L'Art* beneath the caption *The elegant Madame de Beaudreau at the ball*. My parents bought the original from the artist, to be framed and hung in their summer home near Deauville.

I considered my marriage to Émile de Beaudreau a personal triumph. Much was written about the ceremony in the society journals. In the opinion of many social commentators, I had snared one of the most handsome and eligible bachelors in all Paris, much to the envy of many other young women who had eyed him as a worthy catch. I had also won the praise of my father, Gabriel d'Aurevalle. He had long wanted to establish a link – an alliance, he called it – with the de Beaudreau family, prestigious lawyers with much enviable wealth, even more, perhaps, than ours. He hoped Émile and I would help him gain a prosperous footing in the new expanding French empire in Cochinchina. This objective had driven him to persuade the Minister of Foreign Affairs to change Émile's posting from Berlin to Hue.

For my part, securing Émile had been no easy victory. I was obliged to scheme in ways both blatant and underhand, and to flirt outrageously, not only with Émile – well known for his liaisons with beautiful women – but with other men too in my efforts to arouse his jealousy. Flaunting my décolletage was one of my principal weapons. And during my campaign, I enjoyed several brief affairs, one in particular . . . But its details – compromising, as one might imagine – must remain a secret. I regarded what I did as the means to an end in a deadly game. I admit I was no innocent young woman. The fact was I enjoyed being admired and seduced by men, having my physical desires satisfied, thwarting my competitors. But in Émile's case I was the seducer, unashamedly deploying all my sexual tricks to get him into bed. My mother would have been horrified if she had known what I was doing, but not my father, who I am sure was well aware of, and sanctioned, my strategy. For him – an accomplished womaniser – every means, fair or foul, should be tried, since it was in the interest of the family's greater social glory that the union take place. In the end, I had prevailed. With the consummation of our marriage my victory was complete.

The way I behaved felt natural, almost commonplace. Since my earliest childhood I had been used to wealth, as my older brother was – we took for granted the family's opulent Paris house, the large summer home in Deauville, servants to satisfy our every whim, being surrounded by beautiful *objets d'art*. As a young woman with acknowledged striking looks, I was given the means to spend extravagantly on clothes by my father. This lavish lifestyle, the never-ending supply of money, was all I knew, and it underpinned my assumption – so far, unchallenged – that I could have and, moreover, do whatever I wanted, if necessary breaking at whim the rules of accepted social behaviour. My biggest sin, if I had one, was untrammelled pride, taking its lead from my father's arrogance and further fanned by his own success. I recall reading once a remark by the Roman philosopher Seneca: *Wealth is the slave of a wise man. The master of a fool.* I ignored its implicit warning – repeatedly. In hindsight, I was blind to what wealth had done to me. I could not see that the time might be approaching when I would become a fool. The thought was absent from my mind's horizon as I prepared for disembarkation and Émile.

Much to my disappointment, Émile was not present at Saigon to greet me. Instead, a young officer from the Resident Superior's staff, Lieutenant Étienne Tihon, was on the quay to provide his assistance. After an irritating delay at the dockside – mislaid luggage, lazy porters, demands for documents and bribes, the latter deflected with feigned ignorance on my part – we set off by carriage for my new home. It was a rough and at times muddy road, through the teeming crowds at the port, into the heart of the city and then traversing its boundary north into the hills and beyond them to the central highlands. The humidity was sapping, made worse by the heavy, fussy dress I had chosen to wear. The landscape was green, lush and compelling in its strange beauty. My escort made small talk but my mind was elsewhere, on Émile. I longed to see him but he was four days away – some 640 kilometres distant, in the Annamese capital Hue.

After an uncomfortable journey, we finally entered the imperial city of Hue and the grounds of the French residency – the headquarters of the Resident Superior. Passing his mansion and the adjacent administrative office, we came to a stop at a slightly smaller though still impressive house in the same sprawling complex, built in the French style but with distinctive oriental architectural features. Again, to my intense disappointment, Émile was not on the steps to welcome me. His proxy this time was an unsmiling, middle-aged woman, Bui Thi Huong, who swept me upstairs to my dressing room, explaining in clipped French that my husband had appointed her as head of the house. It was clear from her stiff demeanour and pursed lips that she would be an unbending opponent in any attempt I might make to change the daily routine. Adjacent was my bedroom, small and highly oriental in its furnishings – bamboo, bright silks, black lacquer – compared with the spaciousness and luxurious femininity I had enjoyed at home in Paris. Beyond was Émile's dressing room and further along the corridor, his bedroom. I understood from Huong that there was no master bedroom. I promptly decided, regardless of the head of the house, that mine would fulfil that role and be where Émile and I would sleep.

As the servants unpacked my belongings, which disappeared in different directions, I fell asleep on my bed, overcome by fatigue. I awoke to Émile's kiss. Sitting on the edge of the bed, he seemed older, more formal in bearing, more preoccupied. We spoke for a while about my journey and my impressions of what I had seen. Saying he had some official papers to deal with and that Huong was waiting for me to bathe, he proposed that we meet downstairs for supper at eight o'clock.

Bathing involved the ministrations of several female servants, after which I was introduced to the *ao dai* – a traditional long silk tunic, tight-fitting from neck to waist, then split at the sides to form panels that hung freely over the flowing, floor-grazing trousers worn beneath. Mine was red, the trousers white. Under Huong's supervision, the servants measured me for several similar garments, which she insisted I would be obliged to wear in the imperial city, despite my protestations that I was not Annamese but French. According to her, the *ao dai* style dated from 1774 when Lord Vo Vuong of the Nguyen dynasty mandated it as the form of dress at his court for both men and women. Thus attired, I went down to supper.

Émile was waiting for me, also wearing the *ao dai*. I found the table exquisitely set, alight with many candles. A selection of dishes was brought to us in slow succession, dishes whose names and ingredients were new to me, but with which I was soon to become familiar – *to yen*, bird's nest soup; *ga nuong sa*, grilled chicken with lemon grass; *ca kho to*, caramelised fish in clay pot; *goi du du*, papaya salad.

"Tomorrow evening, my darling," said Émile as the last plate was cleared away, "we will dine with the Resident Superior and his wife, Madame Fournier. I understand they have invited some other guests who look forward to meeting you. But tonight you must rest. You've had a long journey and you will need to be in good humour tomorrow."

"I would like to think I am always in good humour," I replied somewhat tartly. Émile ignored the remark. In truth, the prospect of another such meal – or, in all probability, one even more elaborate – so soon, and of meeting the main *dramatis personae* of this new stage in my life when I'd scarcely had a chance to draw breath, had soured my spirits somewhat. But I needn't have worried: the gathering was postponed. Things often didn't happen here when and as expected, I quickly came to understand.

We climbed the stairs, arm in arm. We reached my bedroom but instead of entering he kissed me goodnight.

"Are you not going to join me in bed? We've been apart for three months. I've already told the staff this will be the master bedroom. That being the case, I expect you – my husband – to be with me tonight, to show how much you've missed me, how much you love me. I command it!"

"Monique, not tonight. You must rest, sleep soundly."

"I am your wife, Émile. I have longed to see you, to be held by you. I wish you to show how much you've missed me by making love to me."

"Tomorrow, Monique, I will show you passionately how much I care for you. But tonight you need to rest. Besides, I must attend to some urgent papers."

He embraced me, opened the bedroom door, kissed me again, motioned that I should go inside, and left, shutting the door behind him.

I lay in bed, listening to the sound of the crickets outside and recalling his words – so dismissive. Well past midnight and unable to sleep, I got out of bed and taking a candle tiptoed along the corridor to Émile's bedroom. I slowly opened the door. He had fallen asleep at his desk. As I approached, he suddenly woke.

"Monique, why aren't you asleep as I advised?"

I drew nearer to him. As I did so, he quickly gathered up the papers strewn across the desk and pushed them into a leather attaché case.

"Émile, leave them. I'm not interested in your official papers. I don't want to read them. It is you I want."

He became agitated as he stuffed the last sheet of paper into the case.

"Monique, please, not tonight. Tomorrow. Go back to bed."

"Émile, if we don't sleep together, I will make a scene. Yes, a scene, even at this late hour, even if I wake the entire house."

He looked at me, not in a loving way but with a mixture of hostility and apprehension.

"So be it. We'll go to your room."

"No, Émile, not *my* room. We're going to *our* bedroom."

He locked the case in his desk drawer, stood and started towards the door.

"Come, Monique, let us do as you wish." His words were uttered in an ice-cold, perfunctory way.

As I turned to follow him, I noticed a sheet of paper on the floor near his desk. I picked it up.

"Here, Émile, you dropped this."

He lunged at me, fury on his face. For the second or two the paper was in my hand, I saw from the heading it was a telegram from Paris and that the sender's name was Deveaux. A chill snaked down my spine. Snatching it, he unlocked his desk, put the communication inside, locked it again. Taking my arm firmly, he ushered me from the room, almost marching me along the corridor. We made love but it was mechanical, unloving. Afterwards, he turned away. I lay awake reflecting on what had happened. Émile seemed to have changed. Had I made a mistake to marry him or was he merely adjusting to my arrival in a place where he might still be finding his feet?

In the days that followed, Émile appeared to recover his equilibrium. During the day, I saw little of him as he was ensconced in his office in the Resident Superior's headquarters. On his return in the evening he

would immediately go to his bedroom – in reality, more a study than a place to sleep – and work at his desk for an hour or so. I asked him why he worked so hard. He explained he was assisting the Resident Superior in a delicate mission to fulfil an agreement with the Emperor for France to become the dominant power in Annam, and in Tonkin to the north. It was part of the French government's intention to extend its influence beyond the colony of Cochinchina, thus achieving France's grand aim of full sovereignty in the region. After this hour or so of seclusion, he was attentive and at night we slept together.

Compared with Paris, my daily routine was significantly constricted and at times repetitive. There were fewer people to see; those I did had been sent on appointment from Paris or were expatriates from France who had lived in the country for years and whom I found the dullest. Occasionally I encountered officials from the imperial court. Naturally, part of each day was spent organising the affairs of the household, making arrangements for dinners and answering the many letters and telegrams from family, friends and acquaintances back home in France. I also had fittings for the new wardrobe of clothes Huong had arranged to be made to replace the many clothes I had brought with me, which were either climatically unsuitable or too out of keeping with imperial custom.

On several occasions, Émile travelled south to Saigon or north to Hanoi, either with the Resident Superior or on his behalf. I frequently asked if I could accompany him but each time he replied it would be inappropriate for me to do so. It was necessary for me to stay in Hue.

During one such absence, a telegram arrived for Émile from Paris, delivered to the Resident Superior's office but brought to our house by Lieutenant Tihon. Handing it directly to Huong, he asked her to ensure it was put on my husband's desk for prompt attention on his return later in the day. I offered to take it to Émile's desk myself, but, much to my irritation, which I tried to conceal, she rejected my offer, placing the telegram on a silver tray and insisting on carrying it to his room in person. Since it was beginning to rain, I invited the Lieutenant to take shelter, and to stay for tea. He said he had to return to his office but I pressed him to remain.

He politely asked how I was acclimatising to life in Hue after Paris and for my initial thoughts about what little I had seen of Cochinchina and Annam. I gave him equally polite answers.

"I understand that you and Monsieur de Beaudreau will shortly receive an invitation to join the Resident Superior and Madame Fournier for an audience at the imperial palace," he said. "It promises to be quite an event. The Emperor is a quietly spoken, rather pious man, but he is strongly against foreigners and the Christian religion. As I believe you know, the Resident Superior and your husband are working hard to complete an agreement with him that will cement a more durable relationship with France, allowing the expansion of French influence in this region."

"My husband has not yet told me of this likely invitation. Given his preoccupations – not least the agreement you mention – it must have slipped his mind. Thank you for telling me. I will discuss it with him on his return."

After further pleasantries, he rose to leave. I had one last question.

"I hope, Lieutenant, that the telegram you brought for my husband is nothing urgent, requiring immediate action. Does it concern a government issue or a personal matter?"

"I believe it's a personal matter, madame. It's no doubt another communication from Monsieur Deveaux in Paris. Some are telegrams, as was the case this afternoon, others are letters. Your husband is scrupulous in ensuring that all of his personal communications from Paris are brought here. He gets at least two or three telegraphic messages each week."

I expressed surprise.

"Is Monsieur Deveaux employed at the Foreign Ministry?"

"I do not believe so, madame."

Becoming visibly uncomfortable with my questioning, Tihon made his excuses and left.

I went upstairs to Émile's bedroom. The telegram in its sealed blue envelope rested on a silver tray on the desk by the window. I pulled at each drawer; they were all locked. I picked up the envelope and looked at it closely. Sent from a central Paris telegraph office, it simply bore the date of despatch, Émile's name and telegraphic address, and the word *Personal.* The sender's name was Deveaux. I put it back on the tray and turned to leave. The inscrutable head of house, Huong, was standing in the doorway. She said nothing. After I left I heard her lock the door.

That evening we dined with the Resident Superior and Madame Fournier and some others from the French community. It was an enjoyable occasion, though the conversation was long on bonhomie, stripped almost bare of intellectual content and certainly short on gossip.

Later, back in our own residence, I sat beside Émile. He was relaxed. Putting his arm around me, he kissed me. In response, and to arouse his passion, I removed my long embroidered silk coat to reveal a garment I had recently had made. It was a *yem*, a diamond of cloth covering my breasts, held in place by two pairs of slender strings, one that tied behind my neck and the other across my back. The cloth I had chosen was rich-red silk. Huong had told me that it was considered by many to be an undergarment, often worn beneath a coat or jacket to preserve a woman's modesty. I undid the strings around my neck. The *yem* fell away. I placed Émile's hands on my breasts, eager to entice him.

"You were most attractive tonight, my darling," he said, "head and shoulders above the other women present, including the crusty Madame Fournier. And now you are irresistible, as you were in Paris when you seduced me after the opera. Let us go to bed. I'll join you shortly. Tomorrow is an easier day. I shan't have to leave so early."

He got to his feet, retying the silk strings of the *yem* around my neck and placing the coat around my shoulders.

"Before we go upstairs and I'm abandoned to undress alone, I have two questions."

"What are they, my darling? Perhaps they should wait until the morning."

"No, I don't think they can."

He sat down again.

"Lieutenant Tihon told me today that we are to be invited to an audience at the imperial palace. Why haven't you mentioned it to me? Is it because I have become forgettable amid your daily preoccupations, the lowest of your priorities, or perhaps it is your intention that I should not accompany you?"

"Lieutenant Tihon is quite right. We have indeed been invited – both of us. I am so sorry that it escaped my mind. It is early next week. I will bring details tomorrow evening. And your other question?"

I paused. What would my father do? I chose to ask the question.

"Émile, what is the nature of your business with Monsieur Deveaux? Please tell me. You received another telegram from him today. Lieutenant Tihon brought it to the house. I recall the same name on the telegram you so rudely snatched from my hand the evening I arrived. Huong insisted on taking it to your room herself. She locked the door afterwards."

I recall that moment clearly. His face froze.

"Émile, what is the matter?"

"Nothing," he replied dismissively.

"My husband, that is not a satisfactory answer. There should be no secrets between us. What is a marriage if we don't stand openly, honestly together?"

He flushed.

"Monsieur Deveaux is an acquaintance I met in Paris shortly before my departure. I have been in touch with him about a delicate matter concerning the French state that I wish to pursue privately as it may be to our personal advantage."

"What do you mean, 'to our personal advantage'?"

"My dearest, I am ambitious – for you and me. My post as deputy to the Resident Superior is important but I could do much better. I am seeking sensitive information from a confidential source which may help me to present advice that could lead to an early improvement in my position in the Foreign Ministry. I believe this man Deveaux can obtain the information I require. This matter is highly confidential and I want to make sure that his communications come to me and not to Fournier. I don't want the Resident Superior to know what I'm doing. Since my arrival, Lieutenant Tihon has been under instruction to bring them here, and Huong to take them immediately to my room."

I attempted to ask another question but he pulled me to him and kissed me firmly.

"My beautiful Monique, please, no more questions. We're going to bed – now. My papers can wait."

"Émile, be careful. Don't take unnecessary risks. There are few in this world one can trust, as my father has often said."

And so instead of going to his room, he came to mine – which I persisted in calling *our* bedroom – where he undressed me provocatively as he had done that night in Paris, in response to my tactics of seduction. With no words of tenderness or endearment, he made love to me with an intense passion I had not known in him before but which I relished.

When I woke, early the next morning, he was not beside me. I slipped out of bed and crept along the corridor. I turned the handle of his bedroom door. It was locked.

"Are you there, Émile?"

I heard a shuffling and a moment or so later the turning of a key.

"I thought you were still sleeping," he said. "I'm dealing with a few papers left from yesterday."

"Does that include Monsieur Deveaux's telegram?"

"Yes, I have dealt with it," Émile replied defensively.

Later that morning he left for the Resident Superior's office, a telegram to send in his hand.

As the weeks passed, my life in Hue maintained a regular pattern of boredom, occasional visits to the imperial palace to take tea with some of the Emperor's many concubines proving a notable exception and welcome relief. One woman among them struck me more than the others, from the first time we met.

I remember her vividly: beautiful, young, slim, small, with exquisite porcelain-fine features. Her name was Nguyen Thi Phuong. She told me she was from a family of mandarins connected to the court. Born in Hue, she had been sent at an early age to a prestigious lycée in Paris and later graduated from the École Normale Supérieure. She had returned to Hue highly educated, becoming, she claimed, the Emperor's favourite and most trusted concubine. Madame Fournier confirmed her story, telling me that on the orders of the Emperor, Phuong served as his eyes and ears, not just in Hue but also in Hanoi further north. She appeared to represent the imperial court in many of its interactions with the French administration. In subsequent conversations, Phuong and I talked about many things, her memories of Paris, fashion and art. She spoke about the sexual weaknesses of men, which a skilful woman could exploit to her advantage.

With her encouragement, I adopted more than ever the Annamese manner of dress, dispensing with my corset and full skirts in favour of the narrow-fitting local style, which highlighted my figure. Phuong spoke of other ways to seduce my husband, such as behaving not as his wife but as his concubine, sometimes giving and sometimes denying, teasing, tormenting until he begged. That way, she assured me, a man would easily become the slave to a woman's wiles. Taking her advice, some evenings when I was in coquettish mood I wore the *yem* to entice Émile to pull the strings undone. He frequently succumbed. I began to feel that I was once more manipulating him to my advantage – that I was winning him back. The Deveaux business began to recede from my mind. I accepted what my husband had said at face value. But my peace of mind did not last for long.

My suspicion was re-aroused one afternoon when Émile was in Hanoi. Lieutenant Tihon brought to the house an oblong wooden box, damp and battered. It had recently arrived at Saigon on a boat from France along with supplies for the Resident Superior and his staff. I asked Tihon if it was for me, since I was expecting a consignment of fabric from Paris. He replied that it was addressed to my husband and that the sender's name was Deveaux. Huong materialised as if from nowhere and took the box from the Lieutenant to deliver to Émile's room.

Later that afternoon, while Huong was out, I found the key to my husband's bedroom. On his desk was the box. I picked it up. The content was loose inside. One end of the box had warped open slightly. I tried to prise it further in an effort to see what it contained. Without forcing the lid too incriminatingly, I had the impression that it appeared to hold a tube or canister. I put the end of the box to my nose and detected the whiff of damp leather. Restraining my curiosity,

I put the box down and left the room. As I was going downstairs to return the key, I met Huong coming up. She held out her hand. I gave her the key. She said nothing.

Since Émile was not due back until the following evening, I decided to send a telegram of my own – to my father. I wrote out the message.

> *Please send soonest information about dealings between my husband and Monsieur Deveaux, frequently sending telegrams to Émile from central telegraph office in Paris. Be vigilant in your enquiries and careful in your reply. Monique*

I lay awake most of the night, the draft of the telegram resting on my dressing table. Should I send it or not? I could not decide. After all, Émile had said his correspondence with Deveaux concerned a delicate matter of state and it was surely not my place to jeopardise whatever Émile might be doing in order to advance his career, with its consequent social benefit for me. Moreover, I had not forgotten that it was my father's intention to travel to Cochinchina before long. It was therefore probably wise not to send it. On the other hand, I felt uneasy. What if Émile were deceiving me, and this correspondence was about another matter which he wished to conceal from me?

After breakfast the next morning, I decided not to send the telegram but to keep it a little longer and see what happened.

My mind drew welcome relief from a brief trip on which Madame Fournier had invited me to accompany her, visiting the wives of important local dignitaries but also poorer women, in the villages, observing their humble, harsh way of life. We ourselves were accommodated in a well-appointed hotel in Saigon, to which we returned every evening after each day's excursion. My glimpses of the mighty Mekong River, awe-inspiring though I own it was, made me homesick for my beloved Seine.

On my return, we gave our first lavish soirée at our house, largely for French expatriates. I wore the silk gown I had last worn to the opera in Paris but adjusting it to make it even more décolleté. The occasion was a great success and Émile praised me. The following evening, after a quiet dinner *à deux*, I asked him what was in the box he had received from Deveaux.

"Oh that! They were some documents he had gathered together in Paris for me to see."

"Were they helpful?"

"It will take time to go through them. Look, my darling Monique, I don't want to talk about it. As I said before, it's a sensitive matter. There's an end to it."

"Émile, I observe that when you receive communications from Deveaux you frequently become preoccupied, defensive. Occasionally, there is elation. Naturally, as your wife and out of concern for you, for us, I should like to know more about this matter, to be reassured that what you're doing is indeed in your and our interest, but I accept that's not possible – at least for now – because you won't tell me. But I urge you again to be careful in what you may be doing."

He became irritated and left the room.

A day or so later Émile again left for Hanoi. I went to his room. As usual it was locked but once more in Huong's absence I was able to obtain the key. His desk was free of all papers, as it invariably was, the bookcase nearby well ordered. I opened each cupboard. Everything was neat within. I returned to his desk, trying each drawer; all were locked. As I was leaving the room, I turned to take one last look. I caught sight of a large waist-high vase I had not seen before – on the floor between the desk and the window, partly hidden by the curtain. I went across to look. I admired its ornate oriental pattern. It reminded me of a similar vase I had seen in Phuong's rooms in the imperial palace. In the vase were peacock feathers. I removed one to feel its silken texture against my face but when I went to put it back something impeded its return. The impediment was a cylindrical object. I pulled out a long, slim, well-used leather tube of the sort I had seen artists use in Paris to carry their drawings and canvases. The lid of the tube was secured by a small lock. I tried it to see if it would open. It wouldn't. Thinking I heard movement in the corridor, I put the object back and re-arranged the peacock feathers.

That evening I was puzzled. Why should Émile conceal such an item in a vase? Why not put it somewhere more secure? What did it contain – documents, a painting, drawings? And where had the vase come from?

On Émile's return, I asked, without mentioning the canister, about the vase in his room. He said, casually, that it had been a gift from the imperial palace which he had absent-mindedly omitted to tell me about. Huong had decided to place it there. When I went to his room again the next day, the tube had gone.

With each day that passed, my uneasiness grew. Émile was increasingly preoccupied and secretive and his absences were becoming more numerous, the result, he said, of ever greater demands on his time by the Resident Superior. I spent more time alone, making exceptions for when Phuong asked me to join her, which I always did with pleasure.

As I pondered this turn of events, I received a telegram from my father informing me that in several months' time he would be arriving in Saigon for a tour of Cochinchina and the eastern regions, to promote his business interests. He much looked forward to staying with me and Émile. I replied that we would warmly welcome his visit. At the same time, Lieutenant Tihon announced he was shortly leaving for France on leave, to marry his fiancée; he expected to return with her on the same ship as my father. I decided to entrust to him a personal sealed letter to my father, unburdening myself of my worries regarding Émile and asking him to find out in utmost secrecy what he could about my husband's correspondence with Monsieur Deveaux. I would no longer risk being a fool.

CHAPTER FIVE

Into the Abyss

Of all the women with whom I had shared a bed, it was Monique – tall, svelte, with long, bewitching black hair, piercing green eyes, high cheekbones, strong sculpted lips – who had been the most alluring, the most beguiling, the most scheming. She had flattered my ego, ruthlessly and blatantly outmanoeuvring with her assiduity the many other women who had tried hard to marry me. For her I was the ultimate prize and she had stopped at nothing to grasp it. Every time she touched my hand or glanced at me with that faint half-smile of satisfaction from behind the veil of her hat, she conveyed an irresistible charge of atavistic attraction. Like two magnets in close proximity, she was drawn to me and I to her; the time when we would repel each other was yet to come. As in a medieval sword fight we circled each other to see whose thrust of the rapier would prevail – hers or mine. Would she proclaim herself triumphant because I had succumbed, thereby displaying a weakness in my character? Or would I prove the victor and possess her on my terms? It was a deadly duel with much at stake.

As I confessed to her later, much to her pleasure, I had been forced to concede defeat the night she seduced me after the opera. I had undone her dress and unlaced her corset and she had removed her chemise, but it was by her final, simple action – provocatively unpinning her hair to allow her rich tresses to break free and slowly tumble about her bare shoulders – that she pierced my defence to its core. As I carried her unclothed to my bed, her face – I remember vividly – bore the victor's smile. Yet as she received the proof she had long craved – and which I admit I enjoyed giving – she did not know that in my mind she was not the recipient. It was the girl in the boat – my Marie Desanges – whom I imagined in my arms. I reflected afterwards that perhaps I had been the victor after all.

My parents were delighted that I had married Monique, linking together two wealthy families, each with strong reputations. The Minister complimented me on achieving such an impressive match, one that would, in his opinion, carry me higher in the city's social firmament. He even speculated that I might one day accede to political office. My friends envied me – marriage to a beautiful, rich woman who had long been the talk of Parisian high society. Yet behind my public façade, I was uneasy, unsatisfied. I had secured a strikingly attractive wife but I was obsessed by a young woman I had never met. Unknown to her, she had wormed her way into my mind. I enjoyed Monique's body yet I still could not dispel a profound desire to pursue the unattainable – a beautiful, innocent girl whose fate I wanted to manipulate, just as the goddess Fortuna does, so that she never became the possession of anyone but me. I struggled daily with my conscience. How could I reconcile my marriage to Monique with a longing for Anne-Sophie Courcel? I knew my actions were incomprehensible, reprehensible. Each busy day I fought to keep her out of my thoughts. In the silent hours at night I failed. And now Monique was to join me in Hue. It would become harder to hide my secret.

I was torn by news of her impending arrival. I sought to delay it as long as I could. Not only was I preoccupied with my work assisting the Resident Superior and dealing with the constant flow of instructions from the Ministry in Paris, my obsession continued to burn, fuelled by messages from Deveaux, such as the one confirming he had contrived Alexandre de Mercier's termination of his engagement to Mademoiselle Courcel, or his reports on her activities. Though appalled in my saner moments by my wanton destruction of

her happiness, I nonetheless remained driven to ensure I became and remained the sole arbiter of her destiny, and that one day she would be my mistress if not my wife, in place of Monique, despite the cost and the risk of exposure.

Accordingly, disregarding the steadily mounting sums of money I was paying him, I urged Deveaux to continue his accounts of her whereabouts and activities and pressed him harder to find a means of photographing her. I had to have an image of her which I could look at in my private moments each day. Were I ever to receive such a picture, it would form the centrepiece of my secret archive about her, infinitely more precious than the failed sketches, the artists' and my own, or the communications from the former detective.

I made arrangements for Lieutenant Tihon to meet Monique on her arrival in Saigon and bring her to Hue at a gentle pace, so she would have ample opportunity to see the landscape while giving me more time alone with my obsession. Shortly before Tihon's departure, I received another message from Deveaux advising that an image of Mademoiselle Courcel had been secured and was ready to be despatched at a time of my choosing. I immediately made the necessary arrangements. I had to have it without delay.

Monique arrived, as striking as ever. After taking some time to adjust to oriental customs and in particular to Huong, with her traditional role – and influence – as the head of the household, she gradually settled into her new life. I could see it was not easy for her and from time to time her irritation and frustration got the better of her. Her days were significantly different from the glamorous social rounds she had enjoyed in Paris, where she had always been the centre of attention. I recognised, moreover, that I was not proving a good and attentive husband, that she had found my behaviour towards her on arrival disappointing. I cited work matters as an excuse for my manner, and indeed my dislike of the Resident Superior was partly responsible for my distraction. I considered him a buffoon.

My greater problem – Deveaux – was self-inflicted and was taking its toll. I realised I had entered a Faustian pact. He provided what I sought but his price was becoming ever steeper. Before long it would verge on the extortionate. Although I could afford to pay, I recognised that if I did not end the arrangement soon, there was a growing risk he would demand even more. There was also the risk that, if I did try to stop, he would insist I continue, threatening to reveal my secret if I withdrew. Compounding the problem was my increasing shame that I had lied to Monique about the nature of my correspondence with Deveaux and my failure to keep the correspondence from Fournier. He had already commented more than once on the number of personal telegrams I was receiving, and according to Lieutenant Tihon, he had begun to think that I was plotting his removal so I could replace him. What I had started voluntarily had escalated to an addiction. I had to stop it and resolved I would do so once I received the image Deveaux was sending me.

The day I first saw it is deeply etched in my memory. I returned to our residence towards evening, at the end of a dispiriting trip to Hanoi. Monique was travelling with Madame Fournier on one of those liaison missions at which administrators' wives excel. Huong told me that a consignment had arrived and was on my desk. Suppressing the urge to go upstairs immediately, I poured myself a drink and played a Chopin sonata to remain calm. Huong served supper. I sat alone at the dining table, turning over and over in my mind all that had led to the impossible position in which I now found myself – betrayal of Monique, destruction of an engagement, the risk to my career, my mental turmoil and concealment of a terrible secret. In seeking answers, all I could see was the grim smile on the face of the figure from my train journey to Marseille and the fateful words in my telegram to Deveaux: "Let the game begin." How would the game end?

Pouring myself another drink, I said goodnight to Huong and went upstairs to open the consignment. Inside the external casing, a battered wooden box, I found a slim leather canister which I unlocked, hands trembling, using a key tied to it. The house was silent, apart from the clock in the hallway striking midnight. I slowly removed a canvas, unrolled it and placed it on the desk, securing its corners with paperweights and an inkwell. I gazed at the image – the young, lithe, nude figure of Anne-Sophie Courcel. The painting, measuring roughly ninety centimetres long and seventy wide, was exquisite – the bold brushstrokes, the play of light and shadow on her body, the wistful half-smile on her face as she appeared on the point of turning from the window towards the artist. I was transfixed. The girl in the boat – my Marie Desanges – was here on my desk, in my hands. I ran my fingertips across her likeness. If only I were touching her skin. If only she would come to life and turn towards me so I could see her full beauty. My eye caught the artist's signature in the bottom right-hand corner: Célestine Vauquelin.

As I rolled the canvas to put it back in the canister, I saw an inscription on the back.

To my dearest and beautiful lover Anne-Sophie

Did this mean the painter – Célestine Vauquelin – was the lover of Anne-Sophie? Comparing the handwriting of the signature on the front of the picture with that of the inscription on the back, it seemed a possibility. Was Anne-Sophie already beyond my reach? Had my pursuit, Deveaux's efforts, all the money I had paid been to no avail? Or could a woman who was loved by, and perhaps loved in return, another woman also be loved by, and love, a man? Could that man be me?

The clock struck one. I locked the canister. As it was too large to fit in my desk, I had to find a suitable place to conceal it. Or perhaps I should have it framed and hang it in the house, hidden in plain sight, claiming it to be the work of an artist I had encountered in Paris? But then Monique might ask probing questions about my acquaintance with the artist. I decided to hide the tube temporarily in the vase the Emperor had given me as a gift, amongst the peacock feathers Huong had placed in it. Surely no one would look for it there.

In bed, I couldn't sleep. Two voices competed in my head: mine saying I should let Anne-Sophie go, the other – Deveaux's – insisting on the continuation of our unending contract. Unable to ease my torment, I drank some laudanum. In the morning, there was still no resolution to my turmoil. Later in the day there came another message from Deveaux, asking if I had received the consignment and informing me that as part of his efforts to act on my behalf, he was travelling to Spain in pursuit of Anne-Sophie and Célestine Vauquelin. This journey, he wrote, would require more money, which he required quickly, and fresh instructions.

That evening, with Monique's return imminent, my conscience failed me. I decided to take a further step towards perdition. If Deveaux were to establish that the two women were lovers and thus confirm I could not have her, I would instead, for a short while at least, become a voyeur of their love for one another. I wrote a message to Deveaux authorising him to proceed, agreeing payment in full. Huong despatched the telegram. When she returned to confirm it had gone, I regretted profoundly what I had done. Why had I not been strong enough to end the arrangement? I had the painting. Surely that was enough? But a siren voice had urged me on. Why stop now, if I wanted to be arbiter of Anne-Sophie's future?

Despite my anguish at my weakness, I greeted Monique warmly on her return. We made love that night, and I made every effort to play my part during the Paris-rivalling soirée we gave shortly afterwards, but the guilt of what I had just instructed Deveaux to do almost overwhelmed me. My secret, having to lie, to hide, to conspire and to betray, was becoming intolerable – and increasingly insecure. Monique had been present when Lieutenant Tihon delivered Deveaux's box, and when she asked me what was inside it, her manner equal parts wifely concern, suspicion and disappointment that I was keeping things from her, I almost capitulated and confessed all. Dismayed at myself I snapped at her instead and quickly left the room. Weak man that I was, powerless to heed my conscience and stop the insanity of my actions, I hoped that Deveaux would fail to find the two women, or that his wife might die and that he would be so consumed by grief he would no longer be able to pursue what I had asked him to do. The impending arrival of Monique's father might be a helpful distraction.

Shortly thereafter, I had to travel north to Hanoi again, on government business; I was gone nearly two weeks. While there, as I lay in bed, I suddenly remembered that I had forgotten to remove the leather canister from the vase. What if Huong were to find it, or

Monique? Fortunately, I had the key. But had I locked the canister? If I had not and Monique opened it, what would be my explanation? I lay awake in a cold sweat. I heard Deveaux laughing, as he reminded me that I had agreed to play a game and it was far from over.

CHAPTER SIX

Imperial Illusions

I am Tu Duc, the fourth Nguyen Emperor of Annam, descendant of a proud and ancient dynasty. I reside in my palace in Hue with the Empress and my concubines, amongst whom Nguyen Thi Phuong is my favourite. She is my eyes and ears at court and a clever informant. I was aged forty-eight when she brought this matter to my attention.

First, however, let me acknowledge that, despite my imperial position, I was obliged by weakening authority to concede a significant measure of sovereignty to another imperial power, France, active in its pursuit of colonial expansion to match the empire of the British. It pained me to do so, to be weaker than my forebears, and was much against my better judgement. I do not like the French – I dislike all foreigners, if the truth be known – and I do not welcome the Christian religion in my land. I wish I were sole ruler of my empire but I reluctantly accepted it would not be possible and that I had to play my part in agreeing with the occupiers a sharing of power.

Yet this arrangement, painstakingly negotiated and resembling what in chess I believe is called a stalemate, did not stop me from using opportunities that came my way to put grit into the cogs of the French machine of state, to spoil, delay and disrupt what they thought I had agreed they could have. One way of doing so was to make use of the talents of those around me and to presume on the loyalty of others. That is to say, I insisted that those who depended on me for patronage should play their part by observing, listening and gathering information that might be advantageous. From their efforts, I was able to learn about the intentions and weaknesses of my colonial opponents, which I exploited wherever possible in pursuit of my own ends. The foibles and shortcomings of those sent by France to make their power supreme – their greed, arrogance and ill-conceived tactics – provided rich pickings for me to meddle and scheme. Of even greater use to me was what could be learned about the personal peccadillos, secrets and indiscretions of individual administrators, through loose talk or what they divulged in more intimate moments. The dutiful, clever and beguiling Phuong was peerless not only in the art of deception but also in deploying that skill to expose the darkest of secrets. After all, who could resist the smile of a beautiful young woman or the allure of an invitation to seduce her? Her dissembling charm, her gentle manner and her sorceress's eyes made many men throw away their defences, arrogantly assuming that they could play her feminine wiles and beauty to their advantage. But like the vigilant, stealthy and venomous python, at that moment of greatest weakness she struck.

Phuong first became acquainted with Monique de Beaudreau when she and her husband accompanied the Resident Superior and Madame Fournier to an audience with me at the imperial palace. Madame de Beaudreau's vivaciousness struck a chord with Phuong and after that encounter their acquaintance quickly flourished into friendship, fostered by a mutual love of Paris, where Phuong was educated. They became at ease in each other's company, spending more time together, particularly in Hanoi where Phuong's duties on my behalf often took her. It was during their private conversations that Madame de Beaudreau began to remove her mask to reveal a deep unhappiness, arising, she said, from her husband's refusal to provide a convincing explanation for his strange, confidential correspondence with a Monsieur Deveaux in the French capital, details of which were not disclosed to the Resident Superior, even though they allegedly touched on an aspect of France's policy regarding Cochinchina. According to the madame, this mysterious correspondence – conducted so oddly, always locked away and which Monsieur de Beaudreau was determined his wife should not see – was proving detrimental to their marriage, not least because receipt of a message would affect her husband's moods, ranging from elation to such deep and nervous preoccupation that it had led her to speculate there may be another aspect to the matter, a darker, more personal secret.

Madame de Beaudreau's indiscreet disclosure – few women in my opinion can ever keep a secret – was recounted to me by Phuong one evening when we were alone in my chamber. She suggested that it could be a matter worth exploiting, and asked if I wished her to peel back some of the layers of the onion to see what might lie beneath. I nodded my assent. After all, I never failed to seize an opportunity to discomfit my tiresome power-seeking adversaries. Who knew where her efforts might lead? I recall Phuong's smile of pleasure that I had agreed, of anticipation. I knew she would use her guile to put Madame de Beaudreau at ease in order to discover what her husband might be hiding. If he were pursuing confidential information about the plans of the French government in their dealings with me, that would indeed be priceless. Or it was conceivable he might have a different secret that he dared not reveal to his wife or indeed to his superior. Whatever Phuong might uncover could potentially place Monsieur de Beaudreau in a position where he would be obliged to become an informant in my service rather than have his duplicity unmasked.

Thus I chose to become a player in a truth-finding game but with Phuong as my proxy. As we lay together, I urged her to return to me before long with a good story to share. After all, that is what emperors expect. She did not disappoint me.

That is as much as I wish to impart. It is for Phuong to relate what she uncovered and the ensuing devastating outcome. I shall end my statement now. I have important imperial matters to which I must attend.

CHAPTER SEVEN

Capricious Beauty

My name is Nguyen Thi Phuong. I am, as you will already know, the Emperor's concubine – his mistress – one of many, it's true, but by His Imperial Majesty's own admission his most favoured.

Young, intelligent, admired for my beauty and an accomplished pianist, I do far more than minister to my master's sexual needs. Because of my high birth, my superior education in France (philosophy and art were the subjects that interested me most), my knowledge of the French language and, yes, my skills in the more sensual arts, he has appointed me his eyes and ears at court – in Hue and here in Hanoi. On account of my position, I mingle often with the French colonial administration, so blatant in their unprincipled efforts to exert control over the Nguyen dynasty and the land it rules. I have met many members of the expanding French community – those who have come to exploit Cochinchina. Their greed fills me with contempt. In my master, it provokes anger. During these encounters, I do not offer opinions, hard though it is to restrain my tongue. Instead, I listen, observe and report, and, when my master approves, I plot.

To gain greater insight into my interlocutors and their weaknesses, I use my beauty, my disarming smile and our customs – which, in their hubris, they regard as exotic, intriguing but quaint and unsophisticated – to put them at their self-complacent ease. With this approach, it is unsurprising what a man may divulge, dazzled by an attractive, innocent young woman who appears to hang on every word he utters and to confirm his belief – thoroughly misplaced, of course – that women are eternally dependent on and inferior to men. When I find a prey worthy of my attention and sense him ready to be deliciously indiscreet, I provoke in my victim that irresistible all-consuming desire, using my eyes, the proximity of my body to theirs, the touch of a hand. Those I select for manipulation are frequently easy targets, fruit ripe for picking, almost without exception willingly revealing indiscretions, both personal and political, assuming that the import of what they say will mean nothing to me, a mere woman. What they disclose I write down afterwards with painstaking accuracy and, after careful reflection, decide what to convey to my master the Emperor. He has learned much from what I have told him and he rewards me generously.

Since my return from Paris the information I passed on was of varied quality and a familiar pattern: disclosures about French plans to extend their power. I, a sophisticated young woman, had become somewhat bored by this theme. There was nothing of a more salacious, more compromising, more entertaining nature. Hours at the keyboard practising the intricate notes of Bach and Chopin so that I might play flawlessly for the Emperor offered little in the way of diversion. Everything changed when I met Émile de Beaudreau and, afterwards, his striking wife, Monique. As a tiger sniffs the air for the scent of its victim, I sensed a new and challenging prey which, if caught, might offer juicy meat. The Emperor would be impressed.

I was introduced to Monsieur de Beaudreau, deputy to the Resident Superior, on one of his periodic visits to Hanoi for discussion with the French officials based in the city. He was tall, handsome, polite and engaging – and evidently ambitious. At a soirée, I was able to observe him, to eavesdrop as he oiled his way through the throng. His vanity, arrogance and disdain – manifestations, in my opinion, of generations of wealth spent to selfish ends – were apparent in his every gesture and conversation. Later, seeing him again, I discerned a new dimension to his dislikeability – there was an unpleasant, even sinister, air about

him. His manner was outwardly warm but his eyes conveyed an inner coldness of spirit.

Some months later, not long after her arrival, I was introduced to Madame Monique de Beaudreau. Though we spoke only briefly, I found her lively and engaging, with Paris an instant and compelling topic of conversation between us. Before long, we had the opportunity for a longer and more private conversation. At first, she merely sought my advice on what she might wear to be in keeping with the simpler and more understated style of attire found at the imperial court, in contrast to the fussy French fashion which, she had soon discovered, was distinctly unsuited to her new cultural and climatic surroundings. I encouraged her to experiment – to wear clothes that did not detract from her striking looks and figure. My suggestions echoed what her head of household, Huong, had already proposed; were but embellishments.

As we talked, I detected beneath Madame de Beaudreau's outward veneer of sophistication and self-assurance and her unmistakable pride in her beauty an inner vulnerability, a loss of self-faith, a disappointed woman. Though she did not confess it, I could see in her eyes a dawning realisation that a desire to be desired – a characteristic of many women, I have found – was at risk of being unfulfilled, that what she had fought for might be slipping through her fingers. As I listened to her and studied her face, the more intrigued I became by what lay behind the mask and, moreover, by what might have caused her husband, so soon after marriage, to allow unexplained preoccupations to divert his attention from such a captivating woman so desirous of having her desires fulfilled by fulfilling his.

I set my trap by inviting her to return to Hanoi on the pretext of choosing fabrics and styles for her outfits, so we could spend more time together. This would be my chance to spin a spider's web to snare a victim – either Monique, or a bigger trophy, her husband.

When we met again there was still an insouciant, spirited air about her, yet her eyes appeared darker, sadder than before. Once more we talked, and I encouraged a more informal, personal tone by insisting she call me Phuong. When I asked if she played the piano, she replied, regretfully, "Not well," and requested that I play for her, as she had heard little music since her arrival and missed it sorely. Although her husband was a competent pianist, she said, he was always too busy to indulge her. As dusk was approaching, and with her seated beside me on the music stool, I played Beethoven's *Moonlight Sonata*, a piece my master liked to hear and that might cause Madame de Beaudreau to share her thoughts.

Pausing at the end of the first movement, I heard an intake of breath before she spoke.

"Phuong, you are so calm, so untroubled. I envy you."

"And I envy you, Monique, for your flair and poise. You remind me of all that I admired in Paris. I'm honoured that you should seek my advice on shedding that city's world-renowned fashion for a simpler style of dress. In truth, ours is more flattering, more enticing, especially for someone with your figure. It's rewarding for me when the Emperor responds to something new I might be wearing or compliments me when my hair is pinned in a different way. I'm sure your handsome husband will respond similarly. I would be surprised if you were to tell me he had not."

I could see my blandishments were beginning to have their desired effect, putting her at ease, reigniting her desire to be noticed, to be desired, increasing her trust in me. I felt the moment was approaching when I could attempt to penetrate her inner thoughts. After all, we each have multiple versions of ourselves: a public persona; a more private face when we are with those we trust; and then there is our innermost self, which we do not disclose to anyone – that ocean of dark secrets.

We walked onto the veranda and down the steps to the scented garden, with lanterns hanging from the trees and, in the distance, the sound of gentle, bewitching music from the imperial court. As we strolled the fragrant pathways, I was sure the ambience that evening beneath the stars had been summoned by the divine deity to allow me to weave my magic. I would not fail.

"Madame Monique, let us speak woman to woman."

She nodded.

"You are young, vibrant, your attraction compelling. You are perhaps a little headstrong and used to being admired but that is as it should be. Yet I detect that behind the mask you wear you are disappointed, feel let down, with expectations unfulfilled, no lullaby of heaven. Perhaps I am mistaken. Even if I'm not, perhaps it is wrong of me – a stranger from another culture – to seek to pry into another woman's heart. Still, though our acquaintance is new, I speak to you as a friend. And as the Emperor's mistress and the closest to him, I am used to keeping the most secret of secrets. If you are indeed unhappy and wish to confide in me the reason for your unhappiness, I would be truly honoured to have your confidence."

She did not reply. We walked further in silence and I became aware she was struggling to restrain her emotions. Suddenly, her self-control gave way, tears spilling from her eyes. We sat on a bench beneath a jacaranda tree. I placed my hand on hers.

"Tell me, Madame Monique, what is troubling you?"

"Phuong, I apologise for behaving in such a disgraceful way, for embarrassing you in this manner."

"Madame, you are not."

Amidst her tears, she fell silent once more, evidently trying hard to resolve an inner conflict. She turned to me.

"Since my arrival, my husband has been preoccupied with a curious matter that seems to absorb his attention to the exclusion of almost everything else. When I have questioned him, he says it is to do with his work, his career. Almost once a week – sometimes more often – he receives private telegrams from a person in Paris to whom he replies almost immediately. Often, on receipt of a telegram, he paces the room restlessly, his agitation barely hidden, as though he is wrestling with some destructive inner demon. Late at night, he locks himself in his study, where the messages he receives are hidden. Madame Fournier has told me that even her husband has noticed a serious change in Émile's demeanour. His manner towards me has become abrupt, perfunctory. Before we married, my husband was a man of great self-possession, with a fierce determination if he believed things were not going his way. Now, he seems frequently overwhelmed, almost on the point of defeat, as though by some baleful force of nature. I find his behaviour increasingly disturbing and intimidating. He is no longer the loving man I married so short a time ago. I fought for him, I love him dearly and I will not let him go. But he appears to be in the grip of some diabolical power. I am at a loss to know what to do. To add to my concern, my father will arrive soon. It is important that Émile is in a better humour by then. I do not know what to do."

I took her hand in mine.

"Men are strange creatures. They like to claim it is we who are inexplicable and complicated, but it is they who are often the more unfathomable. When you asked him about the telegrams, did he offer any particulars, who they are from?"

"He will not discuss them. All I know is that they come from a Monsieur Deveaux in Paris."

"Have you no idea of their contents?"

"None," she replied. "They never cease coming, brought to our house by Lieutenant Tihon immediately they arrive from the telegraph office. Every time I see the *petit bleu* envelope my spirits sink. Our head of household, Huong, takes them without delay and places them on his desk to await his return. She keeps the door of his study locked. Recently he received a consignment from this man – a leather canister. I found it concealed in a vase the Emperor gave my husband as a gift. It was locked."

I asked her several more questions, to which she had no answers. We discussed various means she might use to divert her husband's attention towards her, to lure, to satisfy. Slowly, we returned to the house to read poetry together and I played a Chopin nocturne. She willingly accepted my invitation to stay before returning to Hue the following morning. We agreed to meet again soon.

After she had gone, I reflected on what Madame de Beaudreau had revealed. It had greatly aroused my curiosity and I decided I would try to discover more about her husband's preoccupation. To do so I would seek the assistance of the head of the de Beaudreau household, who had once worked for my family and with whom a bond of gratitude and loyalty remained. If she held the keys to Monsieur de Beaudreau's study as Monique had said, perhaps she could provide information that might shed more light on this mysterious correspondence. I sent a message to her.

*

Bui Thi Huong had begun her life of service with my family. My father was a high official – a mandarin – serving at the court of the Emperor's predecessor. Tall, calm, softly spoken, impassive to the point of inscrutability, Huong had learned well the art of supreme loyalty to the imperial order. I remembered what she had taught me in my childhood – obedience. Upon the death of my father, and childless, she had chosen to leave to pursue a more secluded life but I ensured she kept in touch with me. Upon my recommendation, she had re-emerged to offer her services to the new deputy to the Resident Superior. Émile de Beaudreau chose her, expecting his household to be run with great skill, which proved to be the case.

She responded quickly to my message, meeting me clandestinely. After exchanging pleasantries, I posed my question.

"Huong, you and I acknowledge that above all else we owe allegiance to the Emperor. It is to him that we must be loyal at all times. That is what we were taught, that is what you told me often as a child. However hard the test, we must do as we are asked."

"Yes, Phuong, I remember. As you will recall, I served your father, and indeed your mother, with great loyalty always. Shortly before his death, he rewarded my constancy with a precious keepsake, which I wear close to my heart in his memory."

"Yes, Huong, I have seen it. It is very precious and it is an honour to his memory and further proof of your devotion that you wear it still."

Her inscrutable face became wreathed in a rare smile of pride.

"Huong, I ask you on behalf of His Imperial Majesty to serve him in a sensitive matter and without question, just as you served my father."

"Of course I will serve His Majesty, even more so because his request comes through your lips. I regard you as my daughter, and feel honoured by what you have done for me. I would if necessary surrender my life for the Emperor and for you, his beautiful treasured concubine. What is it that you wish me to do?"

"We wish you to bring us certain information concerning Monsieur de Beaudreau."

Her face had resumed its impassivity.

"We wish you to bring us information about the many telegrams he receives – from whom, some idea of their content – and about the replies he sends. We would also like to know what was inside the leather canister he received recently from Paris. As head of the household, you will surely know where these things are kept. The Emperor believes that this information is relevant to the safety of the dynasty. Can you perform this important service for the Emperor? No one must ever know what you are doing, especially Monsieur and Madame de Beaudreau."

I waited for her answer.

Her eyes closed; she sat motionless for a moment or so. Opening her eyes, she nodded her assent. She promised to return soon with information. I was confident she would.

I decided on a further course of action. I was aware of the importance of satisfying a young woman's sexual needs. It was evident that her husband's behaviour was denying Monique de Beaudreau her physical pleasure. I could read it in her eyes. Her desires were unfulfilled. On her next visit, I would introduce her to a young man at court who would lure her into his bed, disarm his way into hers, and thus initiate the pleasure she so earnestly wanted. Such an affair would divert her notice from my intentions towards her husband. The man I had in mind was Pham Thanh Quoc – handsome, agile and beguiling, and another loyal servant of the Emperor. I was convinced that Quoc would easily seduce her, giving her the sexual attention and physical satisfaction she sought. By succumbing to his charms, she would put herself in my debt and therefore be more malleable in the execution of my plan.

Within a week, Huong had shown me the evidence I required. A few days later, Émile de Beaudreau announced that his presence was required in Saigon, giving me the time I needed not only to plot how, on his return, I would secure his acquiescence to my terms, but also to ensnare Monique in my web.

She accepted my invitation to stay at the imperial palace. To help put her at ease, I played Bach's *French Suite No. 2*. I chose it because it reflected Monique's character – her reflective moods, her outbursts of frustrated desire and flashes of imperious hauteur. We talked, and I plied her senses with miniature artworks of food and jewel-coloured juices. Gradually, she relaxed, once more speaking candidly about her hopes and fears. Soon, the time came in the exchange of intimacies to ask the most delicate question.

"Madame Monique, has your husband satisfied your desires recently?"

She blushed in embarrassment but did not reply.

"We said we would be open with one another. Has he given you what you seek?"

"No, he has not. I still long for satisfaction," she whispered.

"Shall I show you how a woman can manipulate a man to provide what she wants?"

She nodded.

I rang a bell. Quoc entered and together the three of us went to my bedchamber.

"Quoc, let us demonstrate to Madame Monique the art of arousal."

He undressed, as did I, and we performed as we had planned. Monique watched.

"Now, Madame Monique, that is what you should do to encourage your husband."

"If only I could, but however hard I might try I do not think that would distract him. His mind is so preoccupied." Her eyes were filling with tears.

"Let Quoc comfort you."

She did not resist as he gently removed her *ao dai* and undid the ribbon holding her dark cascade of hair in place. As he led her towards my elaborate bed, I discreetly left the room, silently closing the door behind me. It was necessary for them to be alone. I knew that if Monique succumbed to him, Quoc would give her the sexual satisfaction she craved.

As for me, I stepped into the garden, satisfied with my skilful ingenuity – perhaps better described as devious manipulation – to contemplate the next move of my chess piece. Later, as dusk fell, Quoc appeared beside me. He bowed and left without speaking. There was no need for him to utter a word. His simple gesture indicated the deed had been done. I went inside, slowly opened the bedroom door. Monique lay asleep, her fine, sculptured limbs barely covered, her face half hidden by her tousled hair. I gently placed a silk coverlet over her and sat beside the bed until she woke.

Over an hour later she stirred. She grasped my outstretched hand.

"Phuong, I do not know what to say."

"Madame Monique, there is truly nothing to say. Reflect on the pleasure you have enjoyed. More will be available if you so wish. For the present, you should rest. You will stay here tonight. I will care for you."

She tried to say more but I put my finger to her lips. I lay beside her as she once more fell asleep. The first fruit had fallen into my lap.

CHAPTER EIGHT

Seville

It was a long, hot summer in Seville, followed by a golden autumn. Célestine and I were sublimely happy in what we considered an earthly paradise. Though beyond our villa in staunchly Catholic Spain we ensured our behaviour towards one another was conventional, above reproach, within the walls of our private sanctuary we could be more open. Her painting flourished, with frequent sales of her sketches, drawings and watercolours of the beautiful Royal Palace and its gardens, and of the equally majestic cathedral with its impressive long nave. In the evenings, we would listen to Francisco's guitar and Sancha began to teach me flamenco, though my body could never be as expressive as hers. On one evening, we stepped back in time and danced an ancient gigue. Visitors to the villa came and went but for at least part of every day Célestine and I were alone, undisturbed. Often while she was out in the city with her sketchbook, I remained in the house writing a diary – perhaps more of a story – about a young woman's choice between a life with a man or with a woman. I also took the opportunity to practise my Spanish with Concepción and Rosario, who came in daily to clean.

At night, Célestine and I lay together, unclothed in the residual heat of the day, reading to one another or sharing yet more of her endless treasure of secrets. She even sketched us, on one occasion me reclining on the bed and her sitting on the edge looking at me as we discussed the nature of beauty; *Two Women in Repose* she called it. As the weeks passed, we grew even closer to each other. For me our friendship had already forged a strong, unbreakable bond between us, physical and intimate, founded on infinite trust. The unalterable fact was that I loved a woman, and was evidently loved by a woman in equal measure. To me – and, I think, to Célestine too – it was not just the fulfilment of sexual desire for one another. It went deeper. Our relationship would of course shock most people were it to be disclosed. Francisco and Sancha were aware of our secret but never referred to it. Outside of the villa we portrayed ourselves as two young women who were just friends and we accepted the compliments and company of handsome young Spanish men.

One was Vincente de Suria – obviously from a well-to-do family – whom I met one evening. He was accompanied by his friend Juan Moreno, who responded in kind to Célestine's wicked flirtation. Vincente and I met several times thereafter. One evening as we walked at dusk in the gardens of the Royal Palace he took my hand and expressed his admiration for me. He said I was the most beautiful woman he had ever encountered. Though taken aback, I was flattered by his words. He asked if he could kiss me. Beneath the fragrant bougainvillea I let him do so. It was a long, lingering kiss but it stirred no frisson within me. We walked on without speaking of what had occurred as though it had never happened. An evening or so later we strolled around the gardens again and once more he asked to kiss me. Once more I let him do so. This time he drew me close to him, his arms around my waist, but being pressed against him engendered no spark of excitement as when Célestine and I were together. The lack of physical chemistry proved to me beyond doubt that, while I enjoyed the company of men and took pleasure in their compliments and flattery, I only felt sexual excitement when I was with her. I tried hard in my diary to express my thoughts and feelings. I wrote that she had helped me to love myself for what I was at a time when I was vulnerable, that we were natural together, authentic. Despite the fact that I was no writer, no artist, she was my muse and exemplar – feisty, vibrant, strong and independent, never accepting defeat or setback. She had shown me what I believed love to be and how to accept it.

As autumn advanced we both knew that our stay in Seville would eventually have to end. The money Célestine earned from the sale of her paintings and drawings, the generosity of Francisco and Sancha and my own dwindling funds would not be enough to sustain us through the winter. In late September, I received a letter from my mother asking me to return to France in time for Christmas, adding that it was time for me to seek a suitable husband and finally hush the lingering tittle-tattle about the end of my engagement to Monsieur de Mercier. After all, my mother insisted, I was a highly marriageable prize, even if I did not believe her. I sent a procrastinating reply which in turn prompted a letter from my father demanding that I end this Spanish nonsense. The letters deepened my despondency at the thought of returning to Paris, of being trapped there in the grey winter with no Célestine for daily companionship. I decided to resist a little longer; just another week or so.

Ultimately, she and I were obliged to concede defeat and arrange our departure from Seville. As part of a long farewell, Célestine and I joined Francisco, Sancha and some of their friends on a trip to Granada to see the Alhambra, badly damaged by Napoleon's troops, and to the nearby Mediterranean coast. It was a remarkable and fulfilling journey. We were absent from Seville for some eight to ten days – far longer than we had planned – because Célestine and Francisco wanted to capture the rich autumn colours in a series of paintings. For me, what I saw and experienced en route to and in Andalucía – the intense sunlight, the enveloping warmth of the day, the ancient architecture, the vibrant colour, the passion of flamenco and the eloquence of the guitar – would be a lasting reminder of profound happiness and sexual contentment. Yet overshadowing these gifts was the impending journey to Paris and separation from Célestine.

An even darker cloud, of tragedy and bloodshed, confronted us on our return to Seville. There had been a violent robbery at the villa. Rosario, who disturbed the thief, had been killed – stabbed to death – as she tried to stop him cutting Francisco's painting of me, the *Mujer* portrait, from its frame. Concepción had been severely injured as she too struggled to stop him. The picture had gone. All that remained was a piece of blood-spattered paper on which were written words we had seen before:

You cannot possess what belongs to someone else.

Célestine, distressed and enraged by the theft of the portrait, insisted the writing was similar to the scrawled hand of the anonymous note she had received in Paris. If that were the case, the thief of *The Mujer* surely had to be the same person who stole the picture from her atelier. She added that there was one other common fact: the subject of each of the two paintings was me. Why should that be? And who was the perpetrator? Before she died of her wounds Concepción had managed to say that her assailant was bearded and had sworn in French.

Two days later Célestine and I, in tears, said farewell to Francisco and Sancha. As a token of our gratitude for their friendship, kindness and hospitality she gave them her remaining pictures, save one small one, which she gave to me.

At the end of our journey up through Spain, my interest in the passing landscape blunted by my low spirits, we crossed the border into France, parting at Biarritz. I was the first to leave. As the train pulled slowly from the station in the early evening, I was suddenly overwhelmed by the weight of my sadness and dread of what lay ahead. I did not want to return to Paris but had been cruelly obliged to do so, leaving behind the one I loved. I had no idea when she and I would next meet. I hid my tears behind my veil. The woman seated across from me in the compartment asked if I were unwell. I shook my head. An elderly man, whose face seemed vaguely familiar but who, in my grief, I could not place, sat in the opposite corner, occasionally glancing at me across the top of his French newspaper *Le Petit Journal*. The front page carried the headline *Hunt for French Suspect in Brutal Spanish Murder*.

Throughout the long journey to Paris, I barely stirred. Others took the spare seats in the compartment, while the man behind the newspaper – wearing a hat pulled down tightly and sporting a thick moustache – disappeared in the early hours of the next morning, never to return, though I thought I recognised his hat ahead of me on the platform at the Gare Montparnasse.

On arrival at home, after exchanging pleasantries with my mother and father, I went to my room, claiming fatigue and promising to give a fuller account of my travels later. In bed, half awake, half asleep, I recalled memories of Célestine in Provence and Seville. In a troubling dream, I reached out to hold her hand but each time she withdrew it, laughing. I reproached her for being so cruel. In the blackest hours of the night I woke and unable to return to sleep plunged into deeper despair. There was no one with whom I could share the secret of our love. Revelation would only bring shame, ridicule and disgrace to me and my family. Yet at the same time I felt consumed by rage that I was forced to suppress my urge to speak of it.

I found the following days hard to bear. Paris in late autumn was cold, grey, wet and dismal – people wrapped in dark shrouds, hidden beneath a sea of black umbrellas. In the evenings, street lamps along the boulevards did little to lift the pervasive gloom. Making polite conversation was unendurable and going to the Bon Marché department store with my mother brought only temporary distraction. I treasured the painting Célestine had given me as a keepsake, of the Alhambra ruin beneath a cloudless blue sky; a whole other world, a different life, captured on a small square of card. When alone in the apartment, I sometimes played Beethoven's *Für Elise*. For me, it symbolised the composer's unknown love. I dedicated it to my spirited lover. If I was particularly lonely, I would play the *Aria* from Bach's *Goldberg Variations*, its gentle, measured notes conjuring memories of the moment in Provence when Célestine slipped into my bed for the first time.

Then one bleak rainy day, I received a letter from Célestine saying that she had arrived in Paris several days before and would write again shortly about where we should meet. Her letter and her coded message of love for me greatly cheered my dejected spirits, even though we would probably have to sit apart – on a bench in the Jardin du Luxembourg, or at the Louvre – to prevent the suspicions of passers-by. Perhaps instead we would meet in the cathedral, where we could sit closer together.

In a happier mood of anticipation, I agreed to join my parents at a dinner hosted by Monsieur and Madame Martin in honour of their son, Pascal, a well-regarded officer in the army, to mark his promotion to colonel at a remarkably young age. My mother insisted on buying me a new off-the-shoulder décolleté dress in flame-red velvet, which she was convinced would make a strong impression on the Martins, particularly their son.

It was an impressive evening, attended by many guests, seated at tables of ten. I sat opposite the young colonel, the table being sufficiently narrow to allow polite conversation. Afterwards, we adjourned to the drawing room to hear a recital of Beethoven and Liszt piano sonatas, followed by the inevitable boring small talk. Although several attractive young women were eyeing his uniform, the colonel seemed to pay particular attention to me and on our departure asked if he might have the pleasure of escorting me to the theatre. Taking a leaf from Célestine's book, I coquettishly said I might be tempted if the play and escort were to my liking. He said he would do his best to meet my requirements and with that he kissed my hand and we parted. In the carriage home my mother beamed with delight at the prospect of her daughter marrying into a well-respected family that had served Louis Napoleon well.

I waited impatiently for Célestine's further letter proposing where she and I should meet. I had so much to tell her and was no less eager to hear her own news. Two days later she wrote to say that we should meet in the Church of Saint-Sulpice late on Friday afternoon, for Second Vespers in honour of Saint Andrew the Apostle. The service would feature music by the church's celebrated young composer and organist Charles-Marie Widor, with Widor himself expected to preside at the *grand orgue*, providing a soul-stirring accompaniment to our reunion. We might even, she suggested, stay and attend evening Mass, enabling us to sit together for even longer, my hand in hers, and perhaps enjoy an aperitif afterwards. In my reply I pressed her to meet sooner, but responding by return of post she was adamant that I must be patient. If we met on Friday as she planned she would have important news to tell me about the theft of the two paintings.

During the next three days, I brought my diary up to date and listed everything I would tell Célestine. I also received the expected invitation to accompany Colonel Martin to the theatre, to see a performance of Molière's *Les Précieuses ridicules*, and to supper afterwards. Under some pressure from my mother, I accepted, despite my reservations about being taken to see a one-act satire poking fun at the manners of young women from the provinces. My mother dismissed my concern.

As I counted the hours to my rendezvous with Célestine and prayed that the precocious colonel would withdraw his invitation, I knew that a difficult decision would soon confront me. Should I reveal my love for Célestine and endure the social consequences of my declaration but avoid marriage to Pascal Martin – assuming, that is, he were to propose and not subsequently withdraw his proposal as Alexandre de Mercier had done? Such a step would mean a life of social disgrace, with no certainty of Célestine at my side. Or should I submit to my parents' wishes and stifling bourgeois convention and marry? If I decided on the latter course, I would be obliged to end my friendship with Célestine and submit to a relationship I would find empty of love and physically objectionable – forced to act a lifelong charade that would cause me profound unhappiness. The night before our reunion, I went to Mass in Notre-Dame with my mother. Listening to the choir's soprano sing the sublime *Et incarnatus est* from Mozart's *Mass in C Minor*, I made up my mind, as the notes soared into the great nave, what my decision would be and that I would reveal it within days.

CHAPTER NINE

An Ill Wind

Taking longer than I had expected, my life in Hue had at last slipped into a pattern of reassuring monotony. I met daily with Fournier to fulfil instructions from Paris to advance swiftly the government's policy to extend its grip beyond Cochinchina into Annam and Tonkin, despite the Emperor's attempts to thwart our efforts. The work I was obliged to do was not to my taste and offered little intellectual challenge. I easily became bored.

In quiet, reflective moments, I longed to return to Paris – not just to become intimately involved in high-level political intrigue but to enjoy the early-evening *plaisirs* the city offered to those with the money to spend retaining the affections of an *amoureuse*, and prepared to risk exposure. My late father – a habitual womaniser and seasoned liar where his liaisons were concerned – had shamelessly indulged in such *plaisirs* for, as he once confided to me, the extra frisson of excitement they brought to his life of law. He showed me a letter a previous lover had written to his wife, which he had intercepted just in time. I retrieved it from his personal papers after his death and filed it with my own. I remember the opening words well.

I am your husband's mistress and confidante. I nod and
smile as he pours me an aperitif while he talks about you,
another expensive gift from him to me on my lap. I am in

*love with your husband. Whether he loves me is beside the
point.*

*We enjoy each other – pleasures shared in bed, secrets
divulged on the pillow – in the apartment he has given me.
But take comfort, Madame de Beaudreau, he will never
leave you for me. You are too precious to him.*

If he pursued such *plaisirs*, then, like father like son as the adage has
it, I wished to do the same. I admired my beautiful wife, and enjoyed
the sexual pleasure she provided, but I still felt trapped. I tried to
convince myself Hue and the work were the cause of my restlessness but
I knew it was Anne-Sophie Courcel. Her image was branded on my
mind.

In the humid heat of Hue, Hanoi or Saigon it was hard at times to
keep my thoughts focused as the Resident Superior's deputy. My
distraction was all the greater because of my resentment towards my
meddling father-in-law, Gabriel d'Aurevalle, for arranging my
appointment to suit his own selfish business interests and without
consulting me. What he had done was unforgivable. Monique's
frequent reminders of her father's imminent arrival further stoked my
animosity towards him.

My life, however, had another dimension: my secret obsession.
Anne-Sophie Courcel dominated every waking and sleeping hour,
particularly those quiet evening moments on the veranda with a drink
in my hand, pretending to be preoccupied with despatches so as to keep
Monique at bay. I would wonder what she was doing, what she might
be wearing and what I would say to her should we ever meet. I felt the
shape of the notebook in my pocket – the black book in which I had
begun to document every detail of my obsession, seeking, in vain, a
measure of relief, of control. I knew the enormous risk I was taking in
not ending my correspondence with Deveaux, which could all too easily
become public, with profoundly damaging repercussions for my
reputation and marriage. We had established a code for our
communications but it was haphazard, barely concealed. Each time I
pledged to end the correspondence another *petit bleu* would arrive,
requiring more excuses, more lies to Monique and more money in

Deveaux's pocket. Then, on the brink of informing him that contact had to cease forthwith and that I would make a final payment as a gesture of goodwill, I received another message.

He informed me that on a visit to Spain to observe Mademoiselle Courcel he had secured another painting of her, more impressive and striking than the one he had sent previously. Given the supreme effort its acquisition had taken, he demanded an even larger payment. Intrigued to see the picture – "striking" suggested it was another portrayal of her unclothed – and to ensure his continued silence, I immediately agreed to pay and authorised my bank accordingly. No sooner had I done so than a second telegram arrived to say that he had received certain information relevant to my intention to seek grounds for the annulment of my marriage. I replied without delay, once more paying a significant sum of francs. I was anxious to have ammunition to counter any attempt by Monique's father to undermine my career further. Moreover, it was better to have the information in my hands rather than Deveaux's. With each communication, each payment, I was wading into ever deeper waters in which I could easily drown. Yet I remained confident I could stay afloat. If it were possible to prove my marriage was invalid, I would be free to pursue my life as I wished it to be.

One evening, after the last of our guests at an unmemorable dinner party had gone and Monique had retired to bed, I sat at my desk not reading the latest instructions from the Ministry in Paris but considering two pressing matters. The first was where to hide my correspondence with Deveaux, now almost bursting from my desk, before the arrival of Monique's father. The second was how best to respond to a private request for me to call on Nguyen Thi Phuong, the Emperor's favourite concubine, whom Monique had met several times to discuss, so she said, fashion and Cochinchinese food. The highly personal request, delivered by the hand of Huong, our head of household, referred to a delicate matter that could not be disclosed to anyone else. While the concubine was a most beautiful young woman and much favoured by the Emperor, she had a reputation for intrigue. What might the sensitive matter be, and why me?

I concluded I had no alternative but to agree to see Nguyen Thi Phuong at a time of her choosing. I wrote to her accordingly, my message conveyed to the imperial palace personally, as instructed, by Huong, the following morning. She returned with a message that I should go to the palace in three days' time at five o'clock in the afternoon.

The next day Monique set out for Saigon, with an escort arranged by Fournier, to greet her father. Her absence from our residence provided the perfect opportunity to find a suitable place to conceal my incriminating communications with Deveaux. I was sorely tempted to burn everything but could not bring myself to destroy any part of this ongoing story of obsession. Besides, it was necessary to have proof of Deveaux's grasping demands for money, which I could portray as blackmail were it ever his word against mine in a court of law.

In the administrative building, I found a large wooden trunk, the kind used for the shipment of personal belongings onboard ship. It was padlocked, but the key was in place. I emptied the contents – assorted porcelain and cutlery – and had the trunk placed in my study. Early the next evening, two days before Monique was due to arrive in Saigon, I dismissed the household staff and began the task of concealment. I laid Deveaux's telegrams and occasional letters in date order on the floor, together with the copies I had taken care to make of what I had written to him and of the payment instructions I had sent to my bank. Then I prepared a series of folders, annotating the covers in a similar style to that used by the clerks in Fournier's office, so that at first glance they looked like standard government filing. Next I took the black notebook from my pocket and ruled columns, entered headings, ready to list each communication, its date and title, a sentence or two about what had transpired between Deveaux and me, and the money I had paid. With everything in place, I sat back, surveying the mosaic of paper at my feet.

It was a laborious process, putting the correspondence and notes in the folders by date and theme, meticulously recording their details in the black notebook. I was soon taken aback by the cost of my obsession, the enormous sums I had paid Deveaux since the first fifty francs I gave him that day in his office. The total was exorbitant. While I had significant family financial assets upon which to draw, the scale of the payments was nonetheless breathtaking and would take some explaining were I ever obliged to do so. I pulled the painting of the girl from its leather canister and tenderly unrolled it. Anne-Sophie Courcel was truly beautiful. I ran my fingers over her image. If only I could touch her skin. Though there was no prospect of possessing her, at least I had ended her intended marriage to Monsieur de Mercier. I was proud of having the power to achieve this result. It was comforting too that, so long as she remained unmarried, there was still a possibility, if I left Cochinchina soon, of seeing her in the flesh, regardless of her apparent female admirer. I put the canvas back in the canister and reread Deveaux's latest message promising that a more striking image was on its way. Looking at the entries in the notebook, the depth of my obsession, its cost and its stupidity, were plain to see. The obsession had become the master, I the servant. But I had no regrets. Why should I?

It was long after midnight when I finished my work, everything filed. The next morning, I instructed the house boys to place the locked trunk in one of the small rooms in the cellar. I insisted to Huong that only I should possess the key to its door.

That evening I returned to the residence early. After reading a telegram from Monique advising that she and her father had begun their journey to Hue, I once more perused the black notebook as a miser looks each night at his monetary assets. It told the story of a frightening obsession which, if exposed, would ruin me. Yet the secret in the book gave me a sense of omnipotence – I, Émile de Beaudreau, son of a famous father and possessor of great wealth, could come to no harm. Undeterred by any obstacle, I was above the law in pursuit of what I wanted. But there remained that nagging modicum of caution and conscience, like a rose thorn, almost invisible to the eye, embedded in one's finger, causing a sharp pain when touched; a reminder of the danger to which I was exposed and the damage my pride, vanity and disdain for others had done to the young mademoiselle. Fournier had enquired several times about the telegrams I received. I had repeatedly lied about their contents, claiming they pertained to Monique's concerns rather than mine. I dissembled to Monique too. What I had done was absurd, costly, and irrefutably revealing of my imperfect character. As I put the notebook in my desk for the night and went downstairs to exude bonhomie over a late-evening drink with Fournier, I realised I had developed a split personality – an exemplary diplomat by day and the epitome of malevolence by night.

I woke in the early hours of the next morning deeply troubled. Something was wrong. I went to my study to retrieve the notebook, flicking through it quickly. As I feared, it contained no reference to my message to Deveaux asking him to find possible grounds for the annulment of my marriage, nor his recent encouraging reply and my instruction to my bank. Had I missed the items as a result of fatigue? I went downstairs to the cellar, unlocked the trunk and hurriedly rifled through the contents. There was no trace of them, even though I had diligently sorted, filed and recorded everything I had sent and received. If they were not in the trunk, where were they?

I was suddenly aware of the presence of someone looking at me. I spun around. Huong was standing in the doorway, a candle in her hand. Its flickering light gave her face a ghostly pallor.

"Have you lost something, Master? Can I help you?"

"No, Huong, there is nothing for you to do. Please go back to bed."

She left the cellar as silently as she had entered it. I rechecked the contents of the chest and without finding what I sought returned to my study to search my desk, in case they had become caught up with other papers. They were not there. I began to panic. Where could they have gone? Had I dropped them? Had someone picked them up? Had Monique found them? Was she now discussing her discovery with her father on their way to Hue? I went back to bed but I could not sleep.

The next day I went as planned to call on the concubine in her small but beautiful ornamental house, which was set apart from the imperial palace. Its design, position and tasteful French style reminded me of Marie-Antoinette's *hameau* in the grounds of the Petit Trianon – her personal retreat, to which she went to escape the pressures of the court at Versailles. I had seen Nguyen Thi Phuong before, but that afternoon was the first time I saw her close to and could fully appreciate her petiteness, youth, her exquisite oriental features and long black silky hair held in place by a highly decorated ivory clasp. Her silk dress was deep blue beneath a red, wide-sleeved overgown. She wore silver-filigreed shoes. Her radiant smile was translucent. As she beckoned me to sit, it was hard to believe she could be as cunning and deceptive as she was alleged to be.

"Thank you, Monsieur de Beaudreau, for agreeing to see me. I've heard much about you and I am sure it has not escaped your attention – observant, well-informed man that you are – that your beautiful wife and I have come to know each other well. We have a great deal in common, not least our love of Paris. Accordingly, we enjoy each other's company, almost as sisters, discussing not only our memories of Paris but matters solely of interest to women." She smiled. Her French was elegant, her pronunciation perfect.

After an exchange of further pleasantries and the provision of herbal tea, I asked how I might help with the delicate personal matter to which she had referred in her letter. She smiled again and leaned forward.

"Monsieur de Beaudreau, I will come to the point. My master, the Emperor, wishes you to perform a service for him – a highly personal service."

"What is it?" I replied.

The concubine looked at me intently. Her eyes were of unfathomable depth, impossible to read; her smile was enigmatic. Her hand touched mine. I felt a chill of fear.

"The Emperor wishes you to provide him with confidential information about France's intentions towards his empire. He thought I was the best intermediary to convey his request."

Her words stunned me. I could not believe what she had said.

"You are asking me to commit treason by providing classified government information to the Emperor? Madame, that surely cannot be. I could not in all conscience do that. It would be unbearable for me, to betray my country and behave so dishonourably. I am sure there has been a misunderstanding. It is better that we bring this conversation to an end."

"Monsieur de Beaudreau, of course you are free to leave. But before you do, please allow me to accuse you of hypocrisy."

Once more I was astounded.

"Please explain yourself, madame."

"You reject the Emperor's request on the basis that it would be dishonourable on your part to accede to what he has asked. Yet it has come to light that you have been engaging in an unseemly correspondence with Monsieur Deveaux in Paris, pursuing certain fantasies and, more to the point, seeking grounds for the annulment of your marriage to Madame de Beaudreau, who is on her way to this city with her father as we speak. Is that an honourable way to behave?"

I was lost for words. I struggled with my reply.

"Madame, my marriage, which I cherish, is a private matter beyond the competence of you or your master. As for the Emperor's proposal, I repeat: I could not divulge confidential documents belonging to my government. I seek your permission to leave."

"Monsieur de Beaudreau, permission is granted. But before you go, I wish you to know that I admire your wife greatly. From my close observation of her I believe she is deeply troubled by your conduct towards her since her arrival in Hue and that she will doubtlessly convey her worries to her father – to whom, I should tell you, the Emperor has granted an audience shortly after his arrival. The Emperor insists on my loyalty to him, in return for which he has given me an honoured place at his side. That is why I speak as I do. It would surely be unfortunate if written evidence of your disloyalty to Madame de Beaudreau were to become a matter of wider knowledge, not least to the Resident Superior and Madame's father. I can imagine the newspaper headlines in Paris about your duplicity causing two families of high social standing to become publicly aggrieved towards one another. It might even lead to a government crisis." She smiled.

"What you are doing, madame, is tantamount to blackmail."

"And do you not already face the prospect of Monsieur Deveaux blackmailing you, to earn more money?"

We sat in silence for a few moments. She merely continued to smile. My secret had been compromised. Someone had seen the correspondence – most likely Monique. Or perhaps it was Huong.

"Come, Monsieur de Beaudreau," she said, taking my hand in hers. Her skin was like silk. "What the Emperor asks is but a small favour. Just some indications of the French government's policy towards him, in return for which your secret will remain undisclosed, giving you peace of mind – indeed, freedom to continue your indiscretion." She held my hand tightly. "You will help, won't you? It is a small price to pay for avoiding any personal embarrassment over the next few days and any graver discomfiture in the weeks ahead."

I nodded assent.

"Good," she replied. "I will inform my master immediately. I look forward to seeing you shortly, to receive the first documents."

I left the palace numb, in shock. I could scarcely believe what I had agreed to do. My obsession with Anne-Sophie Courcel had caused the most pernicious consequence imaginable. There was no way I could retreat. The Faustian pact with Deveaux was now beyond my control.

Two days later I returned to the concubine to give her a copy of the diplomatic code lexicon, which I had illicitly removed from the clerks' office, to enable her to decipher cables from France. With the lexicon, I handed her two recent communications from the Ministry in Paris. She thanked me for my generosity and said she looked forward to receiving further such documents, assuring me that my secret, my actions, were secure. She kissed my hand and put her finger to my lips. Her gesture was unsettlingly sensual.

Two days later Monique and her father arrived in Hue. The following day Monique and I hosted a grand dinner in his honour. Amongst the guests she had invited was Nguyen Thi Phuong, accompanied by Pham Thanh Quoc, another official of the Imperial court. It was an evening of magnificent ostentation.

I engaged in conversation with the guests seated to my left and right but I was remote from the pleasantries, my mind far removed. I was barely aware of the words I was uttering. From time to time I looked down the table towards the concubine. Occasionally, our eyes met and she would smile – the sweet, deadly smile of a victor with its victim in its inescapable grip. Guffaws of laughter came from the opposite end of the table, graced by Monique with her father in place of honour on her right. As Gabriel d'Aurevalle spoke loudly of his first impressions of Cochinchina, and of the abundant opportunities that would flow from a closely intertwined relationship with the French Republic, I realised I despised him. He behaved like a *nouveau riche*, a man without dignity or intellect. As he continued, I looked at Monique, reliving our early romance.

Our relationship was based on self-indulgent collusion in the pursuit of different ends, on differing perceptions. We were each guilty of self-delusion. Most evenings we sought to score points at one another's expense, neither conceding defeat in what had become regular battles of intense verbal jousting. That evening I realised we were two damaged people dancing around untruths against the backdrop of a potentially catastrophic event – my obsession and the heavy price it had begun to exact. All Monique had wanted was to seduce and be seduced by Émile de Beaudreau and by means of her victory become part of my family's dynasty. That evening, in a shimmering gown her father had brought her from Paris, she scintillated her triumph. Now her loathsome father intended to build on that achievement by further manipulating me for his own ends. I looked at Phuong, her eyes lowered as she listened to d'Aurevalle. I knew what she must be thinking and what she would tell the Emperor. As d'Aurevalle continued his monologue, I suddenly felt less guilt for what I had done. One way to stop him, to thwart his intentions, was to provide Phuong and her master with the means to outwit him. She raised her eyes and turned and we looked at each other once more. We both smiled – a smile of collusion. For my part, a more knowing collusion this time.

After dinner, everyone gathered in the drawing room to listen to a recital of Cochinchinese music. For a while, d'Aurevalle was silenced. Though it was late by the time the last guests had left, Monique and her father insisted on a final drink on the veranda.

"Monique, I must say that was a fine evening. I congratulate you and Émile. Fournier was rather a bore, I thought, and his wife not much better. Perhaps I should have a word with the Minister on my return to Paris and get him moved, with you, Émile, taking his place."

"Monsieur d'Aurevalle, I think that would be inappropriate. Besides, Fournier is highly respected and knows more about Cochinchina than I ever will. I have better knowledge of Europe. We complement each other."

"Leave it with me," d'Aurevalle replied.

"Papa, you really should listen to Émile. I'm sure he's right to be cautious."

But her father's thoughts had moved on.

"Since you left Paris, my dear, your mother and I have missed the society gossip with which you so often regaled us – who was up and who was down, all those indiscretions."

"Papa, you exaggerate my wares. What I shared with you were mere fripperies compared to the tales of those with whom you mix – the powerful. I can only imagine what indiscretions they reveal in the boudoirs of their mistresses or in smoke-filled libraries. But then, Papa, you have always been a model of discretion. Who knows what secrets you've heard?"

"My dearest Monique, I do not understand, for one moment, to what you are alluding."

"Perhaps Maman has a better idea. I'll remember to ask her when I'm next in Paris."

Looking slightly uncomfortable, d'Aurevalle changed the subject.

"I thought the Emperor's mistress was exceptional – so young, so attractive, so beguiling. I'm pleased you and she have become friends. Perhaps she will speak well of me to the Emperor. There is much I wish to accomplish on my visit – not just to the benefit of my enterprise but to the benefit of France. We cannot let the British have all the imperial gains."

"I'm sure she will," said Monique, taking her leave.

"Monsieur d'Aurevalle, I too must say goodnight. It has been a long day and there is a lot to do tomorrow."

"I understand, Émile. But please, two matters before we retire."

"Yes, of course. What are they?"

He leaned towards me.

"First, I've told Fournier that I would like you to accompany me when I call on the Emperor. Fournier agreed you should join us."

"And the second matter?"

"I understand from Monique that you are in touch with Monsieur Hector Deveaux in Paris – a former police officer, now a private investigator. She says it concerns a matter of state."

I nodded, gripped by profound fear as to what would come next.

"Just before I left for Marseille I approached him. After all, if you with your connections can trust him with a sensitive issue, so could I. I told him I had a personal matter to resolve and that I hoped he could assist me. He said he would, alongside two or three other cases he's pursuing – one of which is presumably yours. I hope to learn the outcome on my return to Paris. I have no wish to pry into your business with him, Émile, but is he serving you well?"

"He is indeed," I replied.

"Good. Then I shall look forward to the result. By the way, when I asked, he said he knew you but could not comment on what he was doing for you. It struck me that he must be doing well – he was well-dressed and his office well-furnished. His concierge said he had recently returned from Spain – a holiday, I presume. He was tanned but I noticed he had a nasty-looking scratch on the side of his neck, just above the collar line. Enough. I've detained you too long."

We stood and I wished him goodnight.

"I'm glad of this opportunity to spend time with you and Monique," he said, lingering still. "Treat her well, Émile. She's precious to us. I would be disappointed if she were to become unhappy. I rely on you to ensure that does not happen. I know you have much on your mind but she's a fine prize and should be valued accordingly. You will know what I mean. Goodnight to you."

After he left, I sat down. The palms of my hands were damp with sweat. I was on a precipice. One slip and I would fall, a bottomless void below. Should I believe what d'Aurevalle had said? Should I assume that he knew nothing? Or was he already aware of my secret, from Monique?

That night, I could not sleep. I was in turmoil. In the morning, I resolved to bring my correspondence with Deveaux to an early end and to do so with a handsome payment to ensure his lips remained sealed – there could be no disclosure. If there were, I would punish him. My other resolution was to leave my post in Hue as soon as possible and so cease my betrayal of France. Last but not least, I determined that, on receipt of Deveaux's promised information about my wife's background and of the painting of Mademoiselle Courcel he had indicated was on its way, I would seek to end my marriage and my connection with Gabriel d'Aurevalle – and search for Anne-Sophie Courcel on my own, to end my torment once and for all.

CHAPTER TEN

Death in the Rue Frochot

I had become obsessed by money, driven by an insatiable appetite to extract ever larger sums of money from my client, which I knew he could afford. But I was driven too by an irresistible compulsion to expose and ultimately destroy a vain, inglorious and arrogant parasite. As I have remarked before, I saw many of his kind escape justice in my long years as a police officer. Now, my resentment knowing no bounds, I held him in a grasp from which he could not escape, that would only tighten. I would punish him. Moreover, sending fresh demands for money for feeding his voyeurism – one of those appetites that hungers the more it feeds – gave me profound satisfaction. Each payment brought nearer the day I'd be able to afford a large villa in Provence. And if he tried to end our correspondence, I would merely send him more enticements to continue it. I knew that at heart he was weak in character, in thrall to a sexual fantasy I had facilitated and inflamed, not least by providing an erotic image of the young woman he desired to possess. It was truly proving to be a game on my terms – and it was going to plan. I would ensure he got his mademoiselle, but at a great cost to him. Meanwhile, I had to conceal my gains from prying eyes and say little. To the concierge and others, including my remaining contacts in the police force, I remained a modest, respectable ex-policeman.

In hindsight, my unquenchable desire to receive ever greater sums of money caused me to lose all sense. I would now stop at nothing to ensure the proverbial goose kept laying its golden eggs. I disregarded the profound risk I was taking because – so far – it had all been laughably easy. I had stolen the painting of the Courcel girl with no repercussion. Its despatch to de Beaudreau had earned me the biggest payment yet. It would surely be possible to find other baubles to dangle before him, to lure him closer to my viper's nest.

Not unaware of the fact that I too had become a voyeur, I continued to observe the mademoiselle and her friend, Mademoiselle Vauquelin, watching their daily movements and the places they visited together. It was not difficult to uncover their intention to travel to Spain. With adequate money for the purpose and knowing that I would receive yet more from my client in the execution of his instructions, I decided to follow them, leaving my wife in the safe keeping of the concierge, whom I rewarded handsomely. I was confident that I would be able to send Monsieur de Beaudreau a string of reports about their activities that would fuel his obsession and earn me more money. I might even be able to find another personal item revealing more about Mademoiselle Courcel that would titillate his desire.

After arriving in Seville, it took time to decide how best to surveil the two young women in the villa where they were staying. I grew a beard as a precaution against being recognised. It had ample opportunity to flourish: I remained in the city for many weeks, watching, recording their activities in my notebook and sending occasional telegrams to my client – and to the concierge, enquiring after Madame Deveaux's health. I became intimately acquainted with the daily routine at the villa – who went in and out, the movements of the two maids, and when the villa was unoccupied.

The mademoiselles were in Seville far longer than I had anticipated. After a while, I decided to bring my stay to an end: the concierge had begun to ask when I would be back, since my wife missed me greatly and the money I had left for her care was running out. As I was preparing to leave Seville, I overheard the two mademoiselles – out walking one day – discussing their imminent return to France; their money, too, was running out. But first they planned to take a journey south with their friends at the villa. I watched them depart. A day or so later I approached the house, giving the appearance of delivering a letter, which, of course, I had no intention of doing. Peering through a window I saw a large painting on the dining-room wall. What if it were a picture of Mademoiselle Courcel? If it were, and I could steal it, it would surely merit an enormous fee from my client. I observed the villa for another two days, to be sure of the movements of the two maids, Concepción and Rosario. Satisfied, I decided on a time to enter the villa, confident no one would be there.

It was unnecessary to force entry. The doors and windows were open. I simply walked in. What I saw was unremarkable – just another series of artists' ateliers. I entered the dining room and looked at the painting on the wall – the one I had seen through the window. Though the reclining figure had her back to the viewer, I knew instantly who was depicted: the woman the artist had elegantly and skilfully painted was Mademoiselle Courcel. I smiled. I would make my client pay through the nose for the picture.

As I had done in Paris, I took a piece of paper and wrote theatrically the words:

You cannot possess what belongs to someone else.

I lifted the painting off the wall and laid it on the table. Taking a penknife from my pocket, I began to cut the canvas from its frame. I heard a sound and then another. A dark-haired woman entered the room – one of the maids. I almost doubted my eyes and ears. I had checked and double-checked . . . Yet there she was, a carving knife in her hand. As she approached, I seized her arm, trying to force her to drop the knife. She was stronger than I expected. In the ensuing struggle, she fell to the floor, the side of her throat cut and bleeding profusely. The other maid rushed in, also wielding a kitchen knife. We too struggled and she sank to the floor, badly wounded. I snatched up my penknife from the table, hurriedly finished cutting the canvas free of its frame, rolled it up and, stepping over the two bodies, quickly left the villa. To the best of my knowledge, no one saw me leave.

I went back to my lodging and washed the bloodstains from my hands. My only injury was a deep scratch on the side of my neck. I unrolled the painting. The edges, where I had cut the canvas from the frame, were rougher than I had intended but the image was intact and bore no trace of the blood that had been shed. I am no expert in artistic matters but to me it was a beautiful, sensual depiction of Mademoiselle Courcel. De Beaudreau would surely admire it – but at a price.

I remained in my lodging for a day or so to see what happened. There was quite a commotion at the villa, but no sign of any search for the intruder. After shaving off my beard – though deciding, in a moment of vanity, to leave the moustache – and making myself presentable, I began the long journey back to Paris. By remarkable coincidence, Mademoiselle Courcel and I boarded the same train at Biarritz, indeed, sitting in the same compartment. Obviously deeply distressed at leaving Mademoiselle Vauquelin behind, she barely noticed me, only looking up once or twice. With my face obscured behind my newspaper and my hat pulled down, she showed no sign of recognising me as the man who had spoken to her on the beach at Honfleur.

I thought much on the journey about what had happened. The death of the maids had left me numb. They should not have been in the villa. I was sure they were not there when I entered, and I was careless for not seeing them as they approached. Perhaps in old age I was losing my touch. Yet I felt no shame. Instead, I relished, in a macabre and blasé way, reading in the newspaper the report of the killings and the absence of a suspect. It was a relief that so little was known about the perpetrator, that I possessed the painting and that it would earn me a large amount of money. Anxious to be rid of the painting as quickly as possible, I telegraphed de Beaudreau on arrival in Paris, using the simple code we had adopted, informing him that I had a further image of his person of interest, which I was sure he would wish me to send him without delay. As predicted, I promptly received an instruction to despatch the picture and to collect the payment waiting for me at his bank.

*

But the halcyon days of my lucrative assignment came to an abrupt end.

Not long after my return from Spain, Monsieur Gabriel d'Aurevalle came to see me – unannounced – late one afternoon. He didn't need to tell me who he was. I recognised him immediately he stepped into my office, from the newspapers: he frequently appeared in the business and social columns, often commenting about his connection with the de Beaudreau family. Besides, we were not unacquainted. We had done business together before, but always through an intermediary, never in person. I wondered at the reason for this direct approach.

Without invitation, he sat down and, brushing a speck of dust from his expensively tailored coat, asked gruffly if I would undertake an investigation in order to resolve a troublesome private matter. I declined, stating I was too busy with existing clients and suggesting he might prefer to approach someone else if his business was urgent. He replied that his daughter, Madame de Beaudreau, had told him in confidence that her husband was one of my clients. If that were the case, he would wait until I had time to spare. I acknowledged that Monsieur de Beaudreau was indeed a client, but made it clear I could provide no information about his case, other than to say it was a most personal matter. Monsieur d'Aurevalle asked no further questions, though it was evident he was sorely tempted to do so. He sat looking at me with his dark, penetrating cruel eyes. Once again, I insisted I could not help him. Once more, he replied he would wait, and with that he got up, placed his card on my desk and departed. I found his manner chilling.

After he left I was uneasy about the real purpose of his visit. Had his daughter learned of the content of my correspondence with her husband, in particular his wish to seek an annulment if I could find the evidence to use against her? If so, was his call on me a warning to desist? Or was his request genuine, unconnected, merely coincidental? I doubted the latter. Monsieur d'Aurevalle was wealthy, influential and, in the opinion of many and to the certain knowledge of a few, myself included, brutal in the pursuit of his interests.

I decided it would be wise to take immediate steps to cease my correspondence with his son-in-law, conveying my decision in a short telegram early the following morning. He would have little cause to complain. Soon the Seville painting would be in his possession and within another day I would deposit with my bank, for extra security pending his return to Paris, a sealed envelope containing the evidence I had so far gleaned, from a reliable source, about an unpleasant affair Madame de Beaudreau appeared to have had several years previously. What I had learned could well, *prima facie*, provide sufficient grounds for an annulment of their marriage, helped along by an illicit payment to grease the palm of a greedy bishop. Within a week I could close down my business, citing a further deterioration in my wife's health, say farewell to the trusty concierge and take Madame Deveaux to Provence to look for a suitable villa. I had sufficient money in a separate bank account to do so.

The following evening, as I summarised the evidence for de Beaudreau, I received a letter from Mademoiselle Vauquelin that disturbed me greatly.

> *Dear Monsieur Deveaux,*
>
> *I write to you about a most serious matter in which you appear to have been involved to your discredit.*
>
> *A short while ago I encountered a young man at an art exhibition in which I am fortunate to have some of my paintings on show. He was interested in one particularly. It depicts a sunset view of the beach at Honfleur, with a young woman sitting on the sand, a book in her lap, and a man a short distance away, a newspaper thrusting from his pocket. He was intrigued by the way I had portrayed the shadows cast by the setting autumn sun, and said my painting recalled his childhood memories of the beach and harbour. He asked when I had completed the picture, and whether the woman in it was an acquaintance or had just happened to be sitting there. I told him that the young woman was my cousin and the man — the only other figure in the painting — was a stranger who chanced to be walking by. The more the young man looked at the picture the more*

he admired it, saying he would like to buy it when the exhibition ended. I asked his name so I could record it in my sales book. He said he was Alexandre de Mercier.

I'm sure you can imagine my shock. I replied that I was no longer willing to sell him the painting because, unless I had mistaken his name, he had cruelly broken his engagement to my cousin, Mademoiselle Anne-Sophie Courcel, the very person in the picture. I demanded to know why he had done so. I believed a man should honour his promise to a woman, not break it. He was sorely embarrassed by my reaction. Taking me to one side, he said he had been obliged to act as he had done in order to save her family from financial obligations the marriage would incur and which he understood they would be unable to meet. I countered that her family were not only financially secure but also descended from a proud, ancient lineage in Burgundy, their original dynastic seat. I asked on what information he had based his action.

Monsieur de Mercier said he had received his information, unsolicited, from you, a former police officer with, to his knowledge, good credentials. I told him the information he had been given was utterly false and that the ending of the engagement had caused great distress and unwarranted gossip. He apologised profusely and left.

I do not know what may have motivated you to mislead Monsieur de Mercier in such a scandalous, destructive manner, but I request that you write at once to Mademoiselle Courcel's father to apologise for your false and defamatory statement and to offer suitable redress. If you do not, I will report your conduct to the appropriate legal authority without delay. In the meantime, I will inform my dearest cousin of your culpability in this despicable affair.

I expect a reply tomorrow to confirm that you have taken the necessary steps.
Célestine Vauquelin

On reading this letter, I concluded that I had no alternative but to dissuade Mademoiselle Vauquelin from taking the action she had threatened.

I went without delay to her atelier in the rue Frochot. After I had announced who I was, she let me in. It appeared she was working on a new canvas.

I apologised for my behaviour, claiming I myself had been misinformed, and tried to convince her that neither Monsieur Courcel, nor her cousin, need be told. She disagreed, renewed her threat and urged me to leave, insisting that unless I followed the terms of her letter the next morning, she would go to the police. I endeavoured to reason with her but she became angry, even hysterical. Picking up a knife close to her paint palette on the nearby table, she moved towards me, cursing me for what I had done and ordering me to leave at once. I seized the knife and in anger plunged it into the side of her neck. She fell to the floor, blood seeping from her wound. I bent over her to feel her pulse. She suddenly stirred and sought to grab me by the throat, croaking the word *"Bastard"*. In desperation, I pulled the knife from her neck and thrust it once more into her throat. I stood up, aghast at what had happened. Wiping her blood from my hands and the blade, and checking there was no sound on the staircase, I left, the knife concealed in my coat. I snapped shut the padlock on the door.

As I walked, shaking, towards the Place Pigalle, I knew I had committed a heinous crime, but at least what I had told Monsieur de Mercier would go no further.

* * * * *

The examining magistrate looked up from the dossier on his desk.

"In effect, Monsieur Deveaux, you decided, immediately you read Mademoiselle Vauquelin's letter, that she had signed her death warrant and that you would be her executioner."

"No, sir. That was not my intention. I merely wanted to persuade her to desist from what she intended to do."

"I suggest your explanation is incorrect. You went to her atelier minded to take extreme action should it be necessary and, moreover, in the expectation that it most likely would. There was too much at stake. You had already received substantial sums of money from Monsieur de Beaudreau, and you wanted more. Besides, you had already killed two women, in Seville, as a consequence of your arrangement with him. You were well used to shedding the blood of others and vain enough to think that as a former police officer you were incapable of being unmasked."

"If it is decided that I am guilty and should therefore suffer the ultimate penalty," Deveaux replied, "I will take another down with me."

"And who might that be?" the examining magistrate asked.

"Émile de Beaudreau."

"On what grounds?" the magistrate asked.

"Treason," said Deveaux.

The magistrate ignored the audible gasp in the courtroom and continued evenly: "Is there anyone else who may have been involved in the matters about which you corresponded at length with Monsieur de Beaudreau?"

"No, sir," Deveaux replied.

"We shall see if that is indeed the case in the remaining statements I hear. I believe there is more to be uncovered in this sordid and tragic matter."

Deveaux did not respond.

CHAPTER ELEVEN

A Shadow from the Past

"Madame de Beaudreau, what was the real motive behind the letter you wrote to your father from Hue?"

Monique de Beaudreau remained expressionless, and silent. The examining magistrate continued.

"According to what you have already stated, it was to tell him about your husband's growing coldness towards you and the strain this was placing upon your marriage – coldness caused, you believed, by an increasingly obsessive preoccupation with his mysterious correspondence with Monsieur Deveaux, concerning, allegedly, a matter of state he could not divulge."

She did not reply.

"In other words, in order to stop any further deterioration in your conjugal relationship, and to ensure that your husband's career and, potentially, your social position were not damaged by impetuous actions on his part, you wanted your father to discover what the correspondence was about. Once you knew, then you – a possessive woman with great allure, determined to ensure your marriage remained intact for reasons of personal pride and prestige – would confront your husband and, hopefully, resolve matters."

She remained silent.

"In many cases, human nature being what it is, a woman of your evident charm, persuasion, beauty, wealth and ambition would simply issue an ultimatum to her husband. Moreover, it is unusual for a daughter, a married daughter, to share the secrets of her marital bed with her father – with her mother, perhaps, but not with her father. The fact that you wrote to your father to enlist his help suggests to me there is another reason for the letter, which you are unwilling to divulge. That you feared, perhaps, your husband's correspondence was not about a matter of state but about you – about a secret the discovery of which might reflect adversely on you."

"I have said all I wish to say," she replied sharply.

"Madame de Beaudreau, we are investigating serious matters and it is my duty to persist with my questions in order to establish true motives for what happened. Do you understand? You are bound by the law to be truthful, not to mislead or to lie. So, I ask you again. Was there another motive – other than the one you have given so far – for you to write to your father? And, if there was another reason, would he have been familiar with it?"

"I cannot say," she retorted.

"Madame, I'm afraid you must, because I have before me information indicating that there was an aspect of your past of which you did not wish your husband to become aware, fearing his likely adverse reaction if he were and the repercussions that might ensue – an aspect of which your father was already cognisant. I would ask him in person, if he were available to be questioned, but regrettably he no longer is. So, once again I ask you, Madame de Beaudreau, to tell me everything you know. After all, a human life is at stake. In such matters, it is desirable to display a sense of decency, even though this may not be part of your natural disposition."

Monique de Beaudreau looked down. She clasped her beautifully manicured hands tightly together and seemingly struggled to hold back tears beneath her veil.

"Madame, I ask you yet again to answer my question. What was the real purpose of your letter to your father?"

"I believe what you are asking has no relevance to these proceedings," she replied, her tone disdainful despite her evident distress. "It is wrong of you to press me."

"Madame de Beaudreau, it is I, not you, who decides what is

relevant. The more you avoid answering my question the more I am likely to conclude that your letter may indeed shed more light on what happened. So, I ask you for the last time: What was the content of your letter to your father?"

Her posture stiffened.

"If you insist, I will answer, even though in my opinion it remains irrelevant to the case in hand. And what I will disclose has no bearing on what my husband has done. I speak about my own actions without guilt or shame."

"As I have said, the relevance or irrelevance of your disclosure is a matter for me, not you," replied the magistrate. "Please proceed with your answer, madame."

She spoke softly, looking into the distance; a slight smile crossed her face as she began to recall times past.

* * * * *

My father had many *amoureuses*. They were young, attractive, often from the provinces, drawn to Paris by the lure of money in return for providing personal services. My father was not alone in such dalliances. Other men of wealth did the same – it was one of the ways they indulged their need to flaunt their power, or eased the burden of work. My mother turned a blind eye. As long as my father provided her with money to indulge in her own pleasures in life – to purchase paintings and other *objets d'art*, and to give lavish parties – she did not care what he did. Besides, she had her own distractions, fawning fellows who would take her to the theatre and expensive restaurants.

Surrounded by wealth and living in great comfort with servants at my beck and call, I was left largely to my own devices from a young age. Later, I enjoyed the city's social life, able to buy the clothes I wanted and to entertain my friends at home. My mother and father, preoccupied with their lives and loves, hardly ever questioned what I was doing. And anyway, my father doted on me. Whatever I wanted, he gave me.

I was barely eighteen when I lost my virginity. I suddenly felt grown-up, liberated. Afterwards, being in the company of men became an aphrodisiac, further stimulating my sexual desires. When my parents decided to visit Russia – my father was negotiating an important commercial contract – and said they would be away for some two months, I decided that during their absence I would invite people to soirées at our home. Those evenings were sheer fun and they attracted attention in the newspapers. I relished the articles they wrote. I made many friends during this time. When my parents returned, I persuaded my father to buy me my own home so that I could continue to revel in my independence. My mother objected but Papa acquiesced, giving me as a birthday present a well-appointed apartment where I suspect he had once indulged an *amoureuse*.

At last, no longer under the watchful eye of parents, or of servants who'd known me since childhood, I was able to do whatever I wished. I had several brief affairs, which I always terminated when I tired of my lover. It was during this time that I met Madame Roxanne de Cassin, a beautiful, wealthy, always exquisitely dressed woman, some years older than me, who had enjoyed many lovers and who presided over a famous avant-garde salon. Books and art were discussed but everyone knew it was a venue for less cerebral pleasures. We soon became close friends, often spending time together in my apartment, where we would talk for hours before one of her celebrated evenings in the city. I told her of my ambitions, including that one day I hoped to marry someone rich and influential. My father had mentioned the possibility of a "marriage alliance" with the de Beaudreau family. She said she would see what she could do to encourage such a match.

One day Madame de Cassin invited me to visit her at home on the outskirts of the city. The house was imposing, the rooms large and richly decorated. She revealed that many wealthy men came to enjoy the pleasures, comfort and enjoyment she and her young women provided – only, she insisted, to the best of clients. She invited me to stay and watch what took place. I do not wish to go into the details but I sat with her, looking through a grille in the wall at a mirror in the adjacent bedroom in which I could see two people making love. Initially, I was shocked but the more I watched the more enthralled I became – a voyeur in the making. Despite Madame de Cassin's surprising revelation, we continued our friendship – there was something exhilarating about it – and I went to her house several times, little realising that I was becoming obsessed by what I saw.

One evening, at my apartment, she asked if I had enjoyed what I had seen. I confessed I had.

"Would you like a similar experience?"

"Madame Roxanne, I'm embarrassed that you should even think of asking me such a question. Are you suggesting that I should become one of your women? If so, I must refuse, shocked that you think I might be so inclined."

"My dearest Monique, such a thought would never cross my mind. It simply occurred to me that because of your love of sexual pleasure, you might enjoy – just once – the opportunity to be an *agente provocatrice* of illicit delight."

I said I would consider it and we did not refer to the matter again.

A month or so later, Madame de Cassin and I met again at a soirée. Before she left, she whispered that an "important monsieur" was coming to see her the next evening and asked if I would like to join her. I agreed, even though I knew what she had planned. Her reputation was, as I have said, well known, but no one ever commented because she knew too much about the private peccadillos of those who enjoyed her friendship and generosity.

I arrived the next afternoon. With little persuasion, I agreed to perform for her client. She gave me a sleeveless, off-the-shoulder, low décolleté, knee-length silk dress to put on, beneath which was a crimson corset into which she had laced me tightly, and stockings. She pinned up my hair and fitted a mask to hide my identity. Finally, to complete my costume, she handed me fine-leather elbow-length opera gloves. I looked at myself in a large gold-framed mirror surmounted by an ornamental crown. Though I felt a momentary frisson of apprehension at what lay ahead, I admired the svelte, enticing reflection. I was no longer Monique d'Aurevalle but Mademoiselle Delphine, the *nom de séductrice* I had been given. Madame de Cassin then took me to a large bedroom decorated in the Louis XV style – she said it was the bedroom *de luxe*, available only to those of her most prized clients who could afford it. I sat in an ornate golden chair, almost a throne, to await my client. She sat beside me until the appointed hour, a comforting hand on my arm. Looking around I saw a small grille in the wall, opposite the vast, magnificently embellished mirror.

"Are you going to watch me?" I asked.

"Yes," she replied, "but only to ensure you come to no harm."

I will not disclose the name of my so-called client that evening. I recognised him the instant he entered the bedroom – a man of political significance well-acquainted with my father. Without my mask, he would surely have known who I was. He carried me, undressed, to the bed, disappointed I would not reveal my face, and we began intercourse. A powerful politician, paying for sexual pleasure with, unknown to him, the daughter of a man he knew well – the idea gave me profound excitement. Playing the part of an *amoureuse* with skill, I felt a sense of great power over him, should I ever wish to use it for my own purposes. Once or twice I caught a glimpse of myself – masked, naked – in the mirror. I relished my performance and its eroticism.

After the monsieur had gone, Madame de Cassin laced me once more into my corset, complimenting me on my undeniable success. Still masked, I joined her and two other older *amoureuses*, one of whom, with the name Suzanne, was also masked, for an aperitif. The chairs in which we reclined were said to have come from Marie-Antoinette's Petit Trianon palace. It was all utterly decadent, luxurious and voluptuously indulgent. On my way home – a beautiful silver box containing the mask I had used on the seat beside me – I dismissed what had happened that day as mere youthful fun. I felt detached from what had occurred. A young woman, bearing the name Delphine, had willingly explored – and enjoyed – the bounds of sexual activity. Her performance had given me such a thrill I decided that, if I were to marry for love and position, I would wish to be similarly seduced on my wedding night.

Though Madame de Cassin tried hard to persuade me to return, I never visited her house again. After several months, our friendship ebbed, ceasing altogether when she casually divulged *en passant* that my father had been one of her lovers. Before long I had put her out of my mind, though I kept the silver box as a reminder not so much of her but of how one afternoon and evening I had played the part of an *amoureuse*.

Many months later I received an unsigned letter claiming I had been a prostitute within Madame de Cassin's establishment and stating that, if I did not wish this information to circulate in the high social circles in which I mixed, it would be necessary for me to pay an unspecified substantial sum of money. Though I did not recognise the writing, it showed an educated hand. I asked Madame de Cassin to call on me in my apartment, so I could show her the letter. She denied all knowledge. To blackmail her clients or the women who served her was not, she insisted, a practice in which she indulged. As long as her clients paid well for services rendered, the need to do so never arose. Besides, any suggestion that she did such a thing would cause her business to collapse. She had no idea who might have written it. A week later a similar letter arrived, outlining the same terms but adding that, unless I replied within seven days to the poste restante indicated, my secret life would be exposed.

I had no option but to speak to my father. I confessed I had met Madame de Cassin several times at soirées and had accepted invitations to visit her at her home. I did not tell him what I had done there. My father said I had shown poor judgement but being young and exuberant I was hardly to know of her reputation. He said I was not to worry as he would deal with the matter.

"How will you do that?" I asked.

"I have various contacts in the police department – one in particular. His name is Deveaux. I haven't met him and I have no wish to do so. The police are generally corrupt and it would not do my reputation any good to mingle with them. People might form the wrong impression. But through an intermediary we've been in touch by letter once or twice. He's a reliable fellow and gets things done without a fuss. At least, he's proved that to me."

"How will he solve this problem?"

"He's used to this sort of thing. Like any good police officer, he'll be well-versed in surveillance. He'll no doubt arrange for someone to keep an eye on your apartment, watching carefully for anyone attempting to deliver a further letter, and of course an eye on the poste restante."

"But what if there's not another letter? What if the sender goes ahead with his threat to make his allegation public?"

"I doubt if he will do that. There is too much money at stake. Deveaux will take care of it. He'd welcome the business."

"What do you mean by that?" I asked.

"He'll be generously reimbursed for his trouble and for any out-of-pocket expenses he incurs, and I'll make a donation to a police cause. Police officers are paid poorly and I'm always glad to give them a helping hand."

A week or so later my father asked to see me.

"About those letters you received. Deveaux responded to my note promptly. He made some enquiries, discovered the perpetrator and appropriate action has been taken."

"Who was he?"

"Apparently, it was a woman. I don't know the details but everything has been taken care of. Madame de Cassin had nothing to do with it."

* * * * *

Monique de Beaudreau looked at the magistrate.

"I have nothing further to add," she said.

"Thank you, Madame de Beaudreau. From what you have just divulged I draw the conclusion that, as I suspected, the real motive behind your letter to your father was the fear that your husband may have learned from Monsieur Deveaux about the letters seeking to blackmail you on the grounds of your alleged prostitution and, if that were the case, your equal fear that your marriage might be put at risk through your apparent disrepute. Am I correct?"

"Yes, sir," she replied.

"But, given your account, what you did was surely not enough to warrant a divorce or an annulment. You were well aware, before your marriage, of Monsieur de Beaudreau's own reputation for lascivious and unseemly behaviour, just as he must have known of your affairs, about which there was occasional speculation in the newspapers. Neither of you were shrinking violets with regard to promiscuity. You could easily have agreed to tolerate each other's behaviour, past and present, and to keep quiet about what had happened for the sake of your respective family names. That leads me to think there must have been another reason why you feared the name Deveaux. What would that reason be?"

"I do not know."

"I believe you do. And I wish you to tell me."

She gave no reply.

"Madame de Beaudreau, as I have already remarked, the purpose of these proceedings is to establish the truth of what took place and the identity of the person or persons involved. It is therefore imperative that you do not withhold information that may be germane. I ask you again. What else caused you to be so worried when you picked up from the floor of your husband's study a telegram bearing the name Deveaux? If your father were present, I would ask him, but since he is not I insist that you answer."

Her reply was barely audible.

"Sometime later I saw by chance on my father's desk a handwritten note to him saying that the blackmailer had been removed permanently. The writer said he was grateful for the remuneration received but it was best if they never met, and that the matter should be considered closed."

"Did the note bear the sender's name?"

"No, it did not."

"Who signed it?"

"There was no signature, only the scrawled initials 'HD'."

"Madame de Beaudreau, the usher will now show you a note left in the atelier of the murdered Mademoiselle Célestine Vauquelin. From your recollection of the one you saw on your father's desk, did it in any way resemble the handwriting on the piece of paper in your hand?"

"I kept the note I discovered on my father's desk. He searched for it several times and asked me if I had seen it. I said I had not. To answer your question, there is some similarity."

"Why did you keep the note?"

"It gave me reassurance that a stupid mistake on my part would never come to light. I could rest easily. It was written proof that the secret of my escapade at Madame de Cassin's house was safe – dealt with by the police at my father's bidding."

"Did you not feel any guilt that, apparently, a person had been summarily despatched without recourse to the law?"

"I felt no guilt. Why should I? Blackmail is evil."

"Thank you, Madame de Beaudreau. That is all for the present."

CHAPTER TWELVE

The Falling of an Autumn Leaf

Gabriel d'Aurevalle stayed a month. He travelled the region, made trading contacts, met many French expatriates and was granted an audience with the Emperor. But he confessed towards the end of his visit that he was disappointed he had not made better progress and at one point wondered whether he should extend his stay. In the end, common sense prevailed and he decided to embark for France on the date and ship originally planned. Few lamented his eventual departure from Hue.

I had found him boorish and insufferable – an opinion not shared by the Resident Superior, who had spent a significant portion of time travelling with him, dazzled by his money and the prospect of a commercial relationship once his diplomatic career was over – but I kept my antipathy towards him hidden for the sake of my wife, who admired his achievements. Whenever he showed any sign of raising Deveaux's name, I changed the conversation. I was pleased to see the back of him. My wife, joined by the Resident Superior and Madame Fournier, accompanied him to Saigon to say farewell.

While they were gone, the latest mail and other consignments arrived from Paris, brought on the ship that would take d'Aurevalle back to France. Amongst the post was a long slim wooden box bearing the instruction that only I was to open it. I knew instantly what it was – the painting of Anne-Sophie Courcel. I nonchalantly put the box to one side, to avoid any appearance of eagerness on my part to shrewd-eyed observers. It lay on the floor of my study for two or three days. Finally, the opportunity came to open it. It was late in the evening. The house was still and Huong was absent for the night. I gently prised the box open, pulled the internal waterproofing aside and eased out a long slender leather tube. I unscrewed the top and tipped it up. The canvas slid from its casing. It was bigger than I had imagined. Kneeling, I carefully unrolled the painting, stretching it out on the floor.

She was beautiful. The artist, whoever it might be, had created an image that took my breath away. I ran my fingers over the contours of her unclothed body recumbent on a bed, touched her loose flowing hair, covered with mine the delicate hand holding a mirror in which her half-smiling face was partly reflected. I was mesmerised. I do not know for how long I knelt in admiration. Having her before me reinforced my conviction that I had been right to engage Deveaux in a mission of such madness and at such cost. Now I wanted to frame the picture, to hang it on the wall, to gaze at it unceasingly. I could claim it was a work of art I had seen in a Paris catalogue and present it as a gift to Monique, a veneration of her own body. But sanity returned. That could never work. Monique and others would ask too many questions. Better instead to keep the picture hidden from general view, for it to be my secret. I carefully re-rolled the canvas and sought to slide it back into its case. But there was an obstruction. I unscrewed the other end of the tube and pulled out an envelope bearing my name, written in the handwriting with which I had come so familiar.

I opened the envelope. Inside was a letter from Deveaux, stating that before we married, my wife had prostituted herself at the well-known establishment of Madame Roxanne de Cassin and as a result of her activity had become pregnant. Madame de Cassin had arranged for the pregnancy to be ended. Evidence would be made available to me on my return to Paris. He knew this information to be irrefutable because a police colleague had been involved in discovering, at the request of Madame de Beaudreau's father, the identity of a woman who had attempted to blackmail his daughter about her connection with Madame de Cassin.

I sat down to absorb what I had in front of me. In my possession was not only a summary of the evidence I could use in seeking an annulment of my marriage, but also a painting of the beautiful young woman I had first seen in a boat on the river and whom I was now freshly determined to find, to meet and to marry. My pact with the devil had paid handsome dividends. Putting the letter back with the painting, I concealed the tube behind a row of books in the glass-fronted bookcase in my study, locked it and placed the key inside the cover of my black notebook. I sent Deveaux a telegram, written once again in our private code, acknowledging receipt and arranging a further generous payment. I added that before long I hoped to be in Paris to settle final matters – a hint that the arrangement between us would soon come to an end.

A day or so later, on receiving news that my wife and the Fourniers would leave Saigon for Hue the next day, I called on the Emperor's concubine with certain information I had copied from the latest policy instructions issued by the Ministry in Paris. We took tea together and exchanged pleasantries. I told her that I expected soon to return to France and was unsure whether I would be back. It depended on whether I was assigned to a new post. She took my hand and put it to her lips.

"Monsieur de Beaudreau, while I admire your wife's beauty and sophistication, I also have great respect for you – for your bravery in committing to the Emperor's cause. He has asked me to convey his gratitude to you, to which I add my own." She leaned forward, her manicured fingertips touching my cheek. "Though I look forward to seeing you once more before you leave, I wish to assure you now that your secret is safe with me."

"I surely hope so, madame. Betrayal of one's country carries a heavy price."

"Indeed it does, Monsieur de Beaudreau. Why should we betray you, a friend of the Emperor, to the guillotine? But I meant by my remark that your other secret – your obsession with Mademoiselle Courcel – remains safe with me. The Emperor is not aware of it, nor is Madame de Beaudreau. That will remain the case, so long as you serve the interests of Cochinchina in whatever you do and do not disclose the Emperor's efforts to thwart the power of France. I trust you understand the import of what I am saying. What you have done has left an indelible mark upon you."

"I understand, madame. We both have secrets to keep."

"Thank you, Monsieur de Beaudreau, for your assurance. Yours to me and mine to you bind us closely together. Perhaps one day we can seal it with a greater sign of intimacy."

I nodded.

Following her return to Hue, Monique and I became more at ease with one another. But the calm was broken by news that her father had fallen ill after returning to Paris and was now convalescing in a clinic in Geneva. I made immediate arrangements for her to travel to see him. Shortly after her departure for Saigon and passage to Marseille, I received a communiqué from the Ministry requesting my return to Paris to discuss the possibility of a new post. I agreed with alacrity.

Prior to my departure, I paid a last call on Nguyen Thi Phuong, the Emperor's favoured concubine, handing her a list of amendments to the telegraphic code lexicon I had given her before and two new telegrams from Paris. I said I was unlikely to be back, and that it was therefore time for me to say farewell. She replied that there was no need for farewells as she herself was shortly due to travel to Paris, to spend a few weeks renewing her acquaintance with a city she admired and missed so much. She hoped she would be able to meet Monique and me during her stay. I said I too hoped that would be possible.

Having ensured that my administrative affairs were in good order, I took my leave of Fournier and set off for Saigon, taking with me my most personal belongings, including the trunk from the cellar containing my correspondence with Deveaux and the two paintings.

It was a relief to be back in Paris, enjoying the early summer from the comfort of a house in the Tuileries, courtesy of Gabriel d'Aurevalle. Monique joined me shortly after my arrival, from Switzerland, where her father was still convalescing. She confided that he had suffered a heart attack while spending an evening at the home of Madame de

Cassin. Though weak and his business career at an end, he was expected to make a good recovery.

Monique was soon once more at the centre of Parisian society, much to her great pleasure. I, meanwhile, received an early summons to see the Foreign Minister. Congratulating me on the work I had done in Cochinchina during the past year, he told me it had been decided that I should replace Fournier as Resident Superior, but with enhanced powers in order to achieve faster assimilation of the region into the French empire. It was time to bring to an end the Emperor's efforts to block the national interests of France. I would therefore be returning to Hue. I was disappointed with this decision – not least because I knew I would be under further pressure to betray my country – but outwardly accepted it with grace, asking only for a delay of at least three months, to attend to several personal matters. The Minister reluctantly agreed.

To celebrate the news of my new appointment, Monique and I agreed that we should host a lavish evening to which we would invite all our friends and acquaintances, underlining the power and influence of the de Beaudreau and d'Aurevalle families. There would be fine food, a performance of exotic ballet, and dancing into the early hours of the morning. It was to take place in the garden and Grand Salon of the Petit Luxembourg, next to the Palais du Luxembourg, in the rue de Vaugirard in the 6th arrondissement, in August, and would be a social event the like of which Paris had not seen for many years. Monique insisted on organising it herself, to which I readily consented. She intended to invite Nguyen Thi Phuong, to which I acceded also, despite my undisclosed misgivings. Her presence would be a reminder of the extent to which my reputation – and indeed my life – rested in her hands. Beautiful and alluring though she was, the Emperor's concubine was a deadly viper who could strike at any time. From a list left on Monique's desk I noticed that another guest would be Madame Roxanne de Cassin.

Claiming it was necessary to quit Paris for a week or two, and leaving Monique to preside over the preparations for the event, I summoned Deveaux to the de Beaudreau family villa on the riverside in Provence. There I could tell him I no longer required his services.

Waiting for him to arrive, I stood in the open veranda doorway where I had first seen the boat nearly two years before. Behind me, hanging on the wall, were the two paintings, now framed, of Anne-Sophie Courcel. As the house was mine, and visitors rare, there was little risk that the sitter would be identified.

Since the first – and only – time we had met in his office, Deveaux had aged significantly. He was hunched, his eyes sunken and his face lined. We sat in the room overlooking the river. He took in the two paintings but made no comment.

"I wish to thank you, Monsieur Deveaux, for the excellence and confidentiality of your service. You have delivered more than I expected – two paintings and information about an episode in Madame de Beaudreau's life of which I was unaware at the time I proposed marriage. I take it you have brought the evidence with you."

He pulled a large manila envelope from his satchel and handed it to me.

"I think everything you require is there. If you choose to use it in any proceedings, the source of the information must not be disclosed. As I stated in my letter, it came from police contacts. To compromise them would be highly undesirable. You understand."

I nodded.

"Monsieur Deveaux, I have one last request."

"And what is that?" he asked wearily.

"I would like to know the whereabouts of Mademoiselle Courcel."

"Are the pictures on the wall not enough?" he replied.

"That is for me to decide, not you, Monsieur Deveaux."

"Give me a piece of paper."

I gave him a sheet of letter-headed paper from my desk. He took a pen from his satchel and, leaning on a book from the low table between us, he wrote an address. I looked at it. It was in Paris.

"Thank you, Monsieur Deveaux. That has earned you another payment – which must be the last. I will return soon to Cochinchina, but to a new position. Before then I have several personal matters to which I must attend. I believe I can now handle these alone. I understand Madame Deveaux continues to be unwell. In view of the large sums of money I have paid you, I imagine you are in a position to take her somewhere warm."

"So, Monsieur de Beaudreau, is that the end of our acquaintance? I am no longer required?"

"That is indeed the case, Monsieur Deveaux. Except for one thing."

"And what is that?" he asked again, drily.

"I should like to take possession of your files in respect of our dealings. I can put them in a safe place. I trust your discretion, as I have always done. But if anything were to happen to you, I would not wish them to fall into the wrong hands."

"What you're really saying, Monsieur de Beaudreau, is that you wish to remove from my possession any documents I might use to blackmail you or use against you in other ways."

"Precisely so, Monsieur Deveaux."

"There will be a price for that."

"I anticipated as much. What sum this time?"

"I have been to this neighbourhood before, to see for myself the spot where you first glimpsed the mademoiselles, and to pursue my investigations. I visited the small house where they stayed that summer – the summer you saw them on the river from that doorway. I like this vicinity and I would like to spend the remaining days of my life here and give some comfort to my wife. Along the river, on the same bank – about half a kilometre from here – is a house named Maison de Dieu. It's charming – not, of course, as large as this magnificent villa, but it will suit my purposes and I would be your neighbour, a reminder to you of the service I gave and of my knowledge of your obsession with the Courcel woman. I will surrender my files into your safekeeping if you purchase Maison de Dieu for me as a gesture of recognition of what I have done for you."

I was shaken by his proposal. I had thought Deveaux would go away so I could forget him. That would not be possible unless I complied with his request, and yet at half a kilometre he'd scarcely be forgettably "away" at all.

"I am not sure I will be able to arrange such a transaction."

"I am afraid you must."

"Why must I?"

"Because I have killed three women on account of those two pictures on the wall, including Mademoiselle Vauquelin, who threatened to expose me for persuading Monsieur de Mercier to break off his engagement to Mademoiselle Courcel. I could not have that and you, of course, would not have wanted it either."

"And the other two women?"

"Two servants who interrupted my theft of the larger picture in Seville. So you see, Monsieur de Beaudreau, to acquire my files you must meet my request, and accept my presence as a persistent and proximate reminder of the bond of spilt blood between us."

I sat in stunned silence. If I ended the life of this ageing, treacherous man, as I was sorely tempted to do, I would not possess his files and I would be guilty both of cold-blooded murder and of being an accessory to the murders he had committed. I had no courage for such a crime or its consequences. I would have to comply. I chose to do so.

Acting with great speed, within the month I had his files in my possession, locked in the cellar at the villa along with the trunk of our correspondence, which I had transported from Hue, and Maison de Dieu had been purchased in the name of Monsieur Hector Deveaux. As I returned from Provence to Paris with the cellar key in my pocket, I breathed a sigh of relief.

With less than a month to go before my return to Cochinchina as the new Resident Superior, Monique had completed the final preparations for the grand event at the Petit Luxembourg, aided by substantial funds from her doting father and not in the least bothered by my earlier absence.

Finally, the evening arrived: Tuesday the 21st of August 1877. Over two hundred guests attended, all of them, at Monique's insistence, dressed in eighteenth-century costume, in keeping with the history of the building. As she had intended, Monique was the centre of attraction and adoration, striking in a low décolleté off-the-shoulder midnight-blue ball gown with a white fur stole around her pearl-dusted shoulders. Marie-Antoinette would have envied her. I watched her circulate with regal ease and later, when the dancing began, she moved across the floor with supreme poise and grace. Young men – of whom there seemed to be an endless number present that evening – stood in a circle around her, waiting to place their arm about her waist. Like others, I was mesmerised by her beauty. Why should I blemish the reputation of this woman by seeking a divorce that would inevitably reflect badly on me? Her scorn and revenge in such proceedings would know no bounds. Besides, in view of what Deveaux had told me, I could not now risk the possibility of adverse publicity falling upon me. Furthermore, the origin of the evidence I would be required to present in court might be closely examined. I had no wish to disturb the inhabitant of Maison de Dieu. I decided that I would leave matters undisturbed.

As I watched Monique with yet another partner, there was a tap on my shoulder. I turned. It was Nguyen Thi Phuong. I had not seen her arrive. Her tight-fitting off-the-shoulder gown was aquamarine, the revealing low-cut bodice lined in pearl grey. Her hair was pinned up.

"Will you dance with me, Monsieur de Beaudreau? I had gained the impression you were ignoring me. I thought I would see if that were truly the case."

"Far from it, madame. How could I ignore you, the other most beautiful woman in this room? Please forgive me. I have no wish to offend you."

We made our way onto the dance floor. As we took the first steps, she asked me to hold her more tightly.

"A man and a woman should dance as one."

"You dance exquisitely, madame."

"So do you," she replied.

"Where did you learn to dance the waltz with such ease?"

"Here in Paris. As you know, my family sent me here to be educated. I love this city – its sophistication, the theatre, the *joie de vivre*, despite the weather. I love everything about it. I learned so much here. I am pleased that the Emperor allows me to come once a year, to buy clothes and enjoy the fruits of your Western culture – your exhibitions, music, plays."

"Who looked after you during your stay?"

"I had an aunt, but sadly she is no longer here."

The music stopped.

"May I get you a drink?" I offered.

"No. Let us dance once more."

The orchestra began again. There were only half a dozen couples on the dance floor, including Monique with another beau I had not seen before.

"Hold me tighter," the siren concubine insisted.

I complied, observing that a number of women were watching us – with evident envy.

"When we are alone, like this, for example, may I call you Émile?" she asked.

"Of course, madame. As you wish."

"Then I shall do so. In return, you must call me Phuong. That is an imperial edict, which you must obey."

"Why must I obey such an edict?"

"Because, Émile, you are returning to Hue and there we will get to know each other even better than before. I am the Emperor's concubine but he permits me to bestow my favours on others who might attract me, provided my loyalty to him is not compromised. I hope that in the course of continuing the service you have previously rendered to his Imperial Majesty, you might from time to time render a personal service to me."

"And what is that service, madame?"

"To visit my bed, Émile," she said softly. "And if my name does not come from your lips forthwith, I will pretend you have trodden on my foot and declare to everyone you are a poor dancer. So, Émile, stop blushing, hold me even tighter and whisper my name."

"Phuong."

"Excellent," she replied.

As the music ended, she murmured, "I will expect to see you beside me within a day or so of your return to Hue."

With those words, we parted.

In the following days, Monique was lionised in social circles and in the newspapers. She bathed in the adulation. Countless women asked to call on her, eager to say they had enjoyed the company of the queen of the Paris soirée. But then she received a message that her father's health had deteriorated to the point of grave concern and she left immediately for Geneva, to be at his bedside. I decided that while she was away I would return to my summer villa, to reflect on what had happened and what lay ahead. I had compromised my principles – the few I ever had. I had betrayed my country and innocent blood had been shed – all on account of my insane obsession with a beautiful young woman I had seen from a distance but never met. Despite my unalloyed contempt for the wretch I, Émile de Beaudreau, had become, I could not bring myself to remove the paintings, the spoils and symbols of his guilt, from the wall on which they hung so prominently. Anne-Sophie Courcel did not know it but I had become her slave. Each night I wept in despair. Yet the following morning my first act was to view them and to vow that I would try to find her.

I returned to Paris in the late autumn of that year; Monique was not yet back from Geneva, following the burial of her father. Each day for almost a week I sat for hours in a café across the road from an imposing apartment block, the address of which Deveaux had scrawled on the sheet of paper in the summer. The object of my obsession did not appear. Then on the day before Monique was due to arrive in Paris – a Friday, late in the afternoon – I saw her leave the building, walking alone, tall, arresting, poised. I crossed the road and followed her. Eventually, she entered the Church of Saint-Sulpice. I sat two rows behind her throughout the service of Vespers. As it ended, I quickly rose and stood near to the great west door. Pretending to read a plaque, I watched her as she approached, my face half concealed by my hat. She passed close by – the closest we had ever been. Though her face was veiled, it did not hide her beauty, nor the evident sadness with which it was etched. I doffed my hat but she did not notice, her thoughts clearly elsewhere. Somehow or another, I had to touch her, to hold her hand. I had to feel her skin against mine. I followed her for a short while, imagining what my first words to her might be, but in the gathering gloom of evening and the throng of passers-by I lost sight of her. I rushed hither and thither looking for her, but I was forced to give up. She had vanished.

I returned to our house in the Tuileries to prepare for Monique's return. No sooner had I removed my coat than the telegraph boy delivered a *petit bleu*. It was from Fournier, informing me that the trusted Lieutenant Tihon had been arrested. I was to go to the Ministry the next morning, where further information would be provided.

I met the Ministry's head of security. He told me that in the course of a routine documents check, one of the two telegraph codebooks in the Resident Superior's mission was found to be missing, its absence unaccounted for. A thorough search of the administrative office had failed to locate it. Since this particular copy had been personally entrusted to Lieutenant Tihon, and he was unable to explain why it was not in the secure place where such confidential material was kept, the Resident Superior had ordered him to be placed under restraint for culpable negligence and for putting at risk the communications between the French government and its representation in Cochinchina. Unless the book were found quickly, it would be necessary to take urgent remedial steps to avoid the possible compromise of classified information. The Lieutenant would be severely reprimanded and recalled to France for further disciplinary action.

Leaving the Ministry, I walked along the bank of the Seine. I knew exactly where the codebook was – in the house of the Emperor's concubine, where I had taken it. I had foolishly overlooked the likelihood that its removal from the administrative office would be discovered in due course, and that when it was, the official keeper of the book – Lieutenant Tihon, the cipher clerk – would be held responsible. Why should an innocent man be punished for my actions? What was I to do? I could vouch for Tihon's loyalty and honesty, and press the case for his being above reproach. That would be my first step on my return to Hue. In the meantime, I would telegraph Fournier urging him to take no further action. It would also be necessary to alert Phuong, so she could ensure the codebook remained safely concealed. Furthermore, it was essential there should be no indication from the Imperial Palace that the Emperor was aware of the information contained in the documents I had passed to her.

I went to her hotel and waited while a message was conveyed to her suite; she agreed to receive me. One of her attendants opened the door and gestured for me to enter. I sat in an antechamber. A few minutes later I was shown into Phuong's bedroom. She invited me to sit.

"Émile, I never thought we would see each other so soon."

"I have come on a delicate and highly sensitive matter."

"And what might that be?"

I explained. She appeared unworried.

"The book is in a safe place where no one could possibly find it. No one apart from you knows I have it, not even the Emperor. As for Lieutenant Tihon, I am sure your fine words will soon release him from any unfortunate suspicion of guilt."

"That is easier said than done," I replied.

"I have every confidence in your ability to direct attention towards Fournier, one of the least clever men I have encountered."

I rose to take my leave.

"Stay a while, Émile. Let me ease your preoccupations." She crossed to the door and turned the key. "My attendants will say nothing. They are all mute."

The weeks passed. Nothing more was said and nothing heard. Phuong returned to Cochinchina. Monique and I remained in France, pending further news of my intended departure for Hue once Fournier had arrived in Paris. She was preoccupied with the lawyers engaged in the settlement of her late father's estate. It was already evident that, after the payment of certain debts, she would inherit considerable wealth for which she already had ambitious plans. There was much gossip in the newspapers about what she intended to do to consolidate the power and prestige of the d'Aurevalle name, this time solely in the hands of a woman.

Though mourning the loss of her father, it made little difference to Monique's regular attendance at events and soirées – in marked contrast to her mother, who had renounced her pleasures and distractions and was living in black-robed seclusion, not discouraged by her daughter. The aura of Monique's performance – my description, not that of others – at the Petit Luxembourg continued to dazzle the newspapers and social writers. As for us, she and I were together each day but our conversation was confined to pleasantries. The fact was becoming starker: with her father no longer alive to continue his absurd insistence on binding together the two families in a grand social alliance of financial might and political influence, it was increasingly evident from my wife's words and behaviour that she felt less bound to the de Beaudreau name. For my part, I was ever more convinced that before long our marriage would end by mutual agreement, thus releasing two opposites who should never have come together, to pursue their own selfish ends.

Monique's unexpected return to Geneva to finalise some remaining legal modalities provided me with the opportunity to retreat once more to my villa in Provence to contemplate the important decisions I would soon have to make – about the fate of my marriage, the invention of a convincing excuse for declining the post of Resident Superior to avoid being blackmailed into betraying my country further, and how I might finally meet and beguile Anne-Sophie Courcel. It was a relief to be in a place of comfort and seclusion far from Paris where I could reflect on these matters alone. Each morning I would walk along the river bank, recalling the two mademoiselles in the skiff. At dusk I would venture further, to catch a glimpse of the house where Deveaux and his wife now lived. I did not see him but I felt his malign presence. I had become his prisoner but he equally mine – mutual incarceration. We were locked together in our Faustian relationship, trapped by profound mistrust because of what we knew about each other.

I had been at the villa for barely a week when two telegrams arrived. The first was from Monique, informing me with great relief of the completion of the legal formalities, resulting, finally, in the issuing of her father's death certificate. She intended to stay a day or so longer with some friends who also happened to be in Geneva, including Madame de Cassin. They planned to visit the nearby Villa Diodati in Cologny, which the English poet Lord Byron had rented in the summer of 1816 and where he, Mary Wollstonecraft Godwin and her future husband Percy Bysshe Shelley, among others, were alleged to have spent three days together creating stories to tell each other, leading in Mrs Shelley's case to the publication of the Gothic horror story *Frankenstein; or, The Modern Prometheus*. Monique was already imagining the stories she would tell her friends of the villa and the spirits within; my thoughts, meanwhile, turned with empathy to the original Prometheus, chained to his rock. She hoped that I would be waiting for her in Paris because there was much she wished to discuss about decisions she had already taken.

The second telegram was from the Ministry, advising me of Lieutenant Tihon's arrival in Paris for further questioning about the missing codebook. Accordingly, the Foreign Minister had instructed Fournier to delay his own return to France, and to remain in Hue to await the arrival of the Lieutenant's replacement; until Fournier had left Cochinchina, it would not be possible for me to replace him. This latter message increased my unease, further troubled my conscience – or what little I had of one. If the matter of the codebook were not swiftly brushed under the carpet, did I wish Tihon to take the blame for my perfidy in removing the book, to suffer punishment and damage to his reputation when it was mine that should pay the price? Or should I now step forward, take full responsibility for what had happened and face whatever the consequences might be? I could not decide. I looked up at the paintings of Mademoiselle Courcel. There was much at stake – not just for me but for others. Once again I was proving a coward. Surely there was a way out of the situation that now confronted me? My hopes were soon dashed.

A few days later I received a letter from Tihon, forwarded to me post-haste from the house in the Tuileries.

> *Dear Monsieur de Beaudreau,*
>
> *As you may already know, I have returned to Paris for further questioning about the disappearance of the communications codebook that had been in my safekeeping and the risk it poses to the security of our government's correspondence with its overseas missions and representation.*
>
> *I have done my best to shield you from any involvement in this matter. It is evident, however, that my excuses have*

proved insufficient to bring it to a mutually satisfactory end. I therefore wish you to know that for the sake of my honour and the truth, I have decided to reveal that it was you who removed the codebook.

I have the highest respect for you and Madame de Beaudreau and for the efforts you have both made to improve relations between the government of France and the Emperor. There is accordingly much that I would do to repay your kindness towards me. However, for the sake of my family and in keeping with my oath of loyalty to the army and to France, I have concluded I have no alternative but to divulge to the inquiry now being conducted that it is you rather than me who is best able to answer their questions. I apologise profusely for putting you in this position.

In friendship,
Étienne Tihon
Lieutenant

Putting down his letter, I looked yet again at the two paintings of Anne-Sophie Courcel, the woman I had coveted since that day I first saw her, in the boat. Aided by money, influence and the cachet of my name, I had always acquired whatever I wanted in life. No obstacle ever got in the way. Women sought my attention, offered their favours, as Monique d'Aurevalle had done. I thought she would be no different. There had been brief moments when the mademoiselle had been physically close, almost close enough for me to reach out and touch, as on the beach at Trouville or in the Church of Saint-Sulpice. Yet she had eluded my grasp. My thirst for her had gone unquenched. Now my obsession had brought me to the edge of the precipice, a bottomless abyss below. Like Frankenstein, I had created a monster to whom I was in thrall. However hard I struggled to escape, I could not break free from my fixation's iron grip.

I was surrounded by material wealth and the river below the villa was as beguiling as ever in the sunshine streaming from an azure-blue sky. But, as the shadow says, there was no way out for me. It was time to do what I should have done long ago – to admit defeat, to write my confession of guilt, to bring down the curtain on this act of profound folly and to accept that the beautiful creature, there on the wall, would never be mine. She did not know it but the victory was hers. *C'était fini.* It was over. Now I had to pay the ultimate price.

CHAPTER THIRTEEN

A Bitter Harvest

When Friday came, I went to the Church of Saint-Sulpice at the time Célestine and I had agreed, the early evening. We had been to the church several times before. It was a public place, of course, but, for us, equally private – the congregation looked towards the priest and the high altar, and were preoccupied with personal thoughts, or transported by the magnificent sounds of the Cavaillé-Coll organs and the choir, rather than observing those around them. Surrounded by many we would sit beside one another, my hand touching hers surreptitiously. We would sometimes pass secret love notes to one another, written on scraps of paper, which we would put in our pocket to be read later. You might think such actions childish but with opportunities to be alone so infrequent, it was one of the few means available to express our intimate sentiments towards one another. The room where she lodged offered no privacy to share her bed. If we went to a café afterwards, there might be a street corner shrouded in shadow where we could share an illicit kiss and whisper our love for one another.

I was looking forward so much to seeing Célestine that day, to sitting beside her during Vespers, having an aperitif together afterwards, and hearing the news she had promised to tell me about the stolen paintings. I also hoped to try to persuade her that we should go once more to Honfleur, where we could be physically close, provided, of course, she had earned enough money from the sale of her paintings at the salon currently exhibiting them. I was so eager to see her that I arrived at the church early, to ensure we could sit in our familiar pew near the front of the nave, close to where the pious knelt. As I have said, on their knees they would not observe the exchange of notes, our hands touching or our silently mouthed words of love to one another. Célestine was always punctual but, on this occasion, she was uncharacteristically late. The bell rang for the commencement of Vespers but still there was no sign of her. I barely registered the glorious antiphonal offerings of the choir, delivered up from behind the high altar, or the all-enveloping resonance of the *grand orgue*, enriched by the smaller *orgue de choeur* in the chancel, and throughout prayers I tried to think what could have delayed her. At the end of the service, I quickly left the church expecting to see her on the steps but she was not there. I walked home quickly, hoping I would perhaps encounter her on the way, or find a note delivered to the concierge explaining her absence. There was none. I wanted to go to her atelier but my mother prevailed on me to stay to join her and some of her friends to discuss a recently published book about Racine. Besides, my mother insisted that it was too late for a young woman to be seen alone around the Place Pigalle. In that notorious area, some might think I was a prostitute.

The next morning there was still no letter from Célestine. I decided that I would go first to the salon. I was ready to scold her for her insensitivity in forgetting our rendezvous the previous evening, but she was not there and, according to those in the adjacent booth, she had not been there for two days. I looked at the half dozen of Célestine's paintings on display, which included the one she had painted during our weekend together in Honfleur, a small one of the cathedral in Seville, and a self-portrait I had not seen before. She was looking directly at the viewer, her long tousled chestnut-red hair framing the beautiful face I admired so much. It was tinged with a slight trace of melancholy. A large bow of white silk rested nonchalantly at her throat, and a brown cape was cast casually around her shoulders. This was the woman I loved but could not find. I longed to touch her face.

Lost in thought, I was unaware of the salon owner, Monsieur Tessier, standing beside me.

"It's a remarkable self-portrait. So lifelike, is it not? Several people have stopped to gaze at it and also at the painting of the beach at Honfleur. I, like many others, think it captures the late-afternoon sun to perfection."

"I'm the woman on the beach. I was there when Mademoiselle Vauquelin painted it. This is the first time I've seen it completed."

"And your name is . . . ?"

"Mademoiselle Anne-Sophie Courcel. The artist is my cousin. We hardly knew each other in childhood but now we have become close friends."

"Mademoiselle Courcel, I should be most grateful if you would find your cousin and request that she please return to the salon without further delay. There is a monsieur who has shown great interest in one of these paintings, and still wishes to buy it, despite Mademoiselle Vauquelin's earlier reluctance to sell it to him. It would be a great pity if the exhibition were to end without an agreement being reached."

"Which painting was he interested in?"

"The scene at Honfleur. He told me the woman on the beach reminded him of someone to whom he owed an apology for listening to some malevolent advice. He became quite agitated about it. Yesterday was the third time he's come, hoping to talk once more to Mademoiselle Vauquelin. Here's the card he left: Monsieur Alexandre de Mercier. So, Mademoiselle Courcel, I hope you can find your cousin and persuade her to return and speak to Monsieur de Mercier, and at the same time, perhaps, hear more about the apology he feels he owes."

"I will see what I can do."

I quickly left the salon. I decided to go to Célestine's atelier in the hope she might be there. If she wasn't, I would have to find the room in which she boarded. I had never been there but I knew roughly where it was. As I hurried to the rue Frochot, more worried than ever about Célestine's disappearance, I wondered about the nature of the apology Alexandre de Mercier felt he owed, the woman to whom he owed it, of whom my likeness in the painting reminded him, and the advice that had warranted it. Was she the victim of another unexpectedly and callously ended engagement, perhaps? What advice could possibly justify causing so much distress and embarrassment to her family – or to mine?

It was early afternoon when I arrived in the rue Frochot. After walking up and down the street several times, deciding how much I should chastise Célestine, I entered the building. There were several ateliers – hers was on the top floor, smaller than the others but with bigger windows, giving her more light. I had been there a handful of times before, to see some of her work and to sit together discussing our vague plans to run away for the rest of our lives. The door was padlocked. Anxious to see whether Célestine had left a letter for me inside, revealing her whereabouts, I opened my purse and took out the spare key she had given me for safe keeping. Releasing the padlock, I slowly opened the door.

The shutters on the large windows were closed and a table on which she kept her collection of paints and rested her palette was tipped on its side. I opened the door further and stepped inside. Then I saw her motionless on the floor. I will never erase that image from my mind. My beautiful Célestine lay on her back, her head twisted to one side, two large wounds in her neck, her hair matted with congealed blood. Her eyes were still open, her face contorted with fury. I screamed. I cannot remember exactly what happened next but someone – probably from the floor below – rushed in as I fell to the floor. I recall the police arriving as I was helped to my feet. They escorted me from the building and took me to the Pigalle police station where they began to question me. Though deeply distressed, I did my best to answer their persistent barrage. It was some hours later when they allowed my father to take me home. There were reporters outside the police station who crowded around us. We had to push our way through them to the waiting carriage. My mother summoned a doctor and for the next two days I was heavily sedated. My father has told me that during this time, newspapers such as *Le Petit Journal* carried vivid headlines: *Une artiste meurt, attaquée brutalement au couteau* and *Affreux carnage rue Frochot*. Another newspaper had the headline, *On suspecte une jeune femme de ce crime passionel,* and yet another, *Elle est arrêtée pour meurtre de la rue Frochot.* A reporter even pestered our concierge with questions about me, but she drove him away.

Refusing further sedation, I left our apartment the following day, while my parents were out, to go to the salon. I told Monsieur Tessier that I had come to collect Célestine's paintings, and that my family would pay any costs he might be owed. Expressing deep sympathy, he said that payment would not be necessary and began to help me remove the paintings from the wall. As we were doing so, a voice spoke from behind. It was Alexandre de Mercier.

"Mademoiselle Courcel, I convey to you my sincerest condolences on the brutal death of your cousin, Mademoiselle Vauquelin. I loved the Honfleur picture you have taken down. Not only was it exquisitely executed, it was a reminder of you."

"Why should you wish to be reminded of me?" I replied sharply.

"Monsieur Tessier, have you a private room where I might speak to Mademoiselle Courcel alone for a few minutes?"

"That is not necessary, Monsieur Tessier. There is nothing Monsieur Mercier can say to assuage my grief at my cousin's murder or my anger towards him."

"Mademoiselle, I acknowledge I cannot allay your grief for a cousin to whom it is clear you were devoted, but there is another matter about which I wish to speak. I beg you to hear me out."

Though I had no interest in hearing what he wanted to say, I reluctantly agreed, not least because our heated conversation was beginning to attract attention. No sooner had Monsieur Tessier shown us into a small side room – usually used for conducting delicate sales negotiations, he explained – than Alexandre de Mercier turned earnestly towards me.

"Mademoiselle Courcel, I deeply regret the termination of our engagement. I treated you and your family abominably. I thought I was doing it for the best of motives – to spare your family grave financial embarrassment."

"What financial embarrassment?"

"First, let me say that, though I loved you and admired your beauty, I found it hard to express my sentiments. While plucking up the courage to be bolder, I received information – in writing and apparently from a reliable source – that your family had significant debts and that the cost of our marriage would place an intolerable burden upon you. I decided, in the light of that information, that it would be best to end our engagement, without undue specification of the reason."

"Monsieur de Mercier, that information was utterly false. Tell me, did you really break our engagement to spare my family so-called embarrassment, or was it more to preserve your own self-righteous reputation? And from whom, might I ask, did you receive this malicious information? Did you not question its veracity, confront the author?"

"It came unsolicited, as I explained to your late cousin, from a former senior police officer, Monsieur Hector Deveaux, apparently highly respected. I believed it. In the circumstances, at the time, I thought I was acting in the best interests of you and your family. I now know that wasn't the case, for which I am utterly remorseful."

"Monsieur de Mercier, you behaved despicably. On hearing such a rumour, you should have had the courage to raise your concern with me, not to accept the tittle-tattle of some retired policeman. It displays poor judgement on your part and I'm glad that our engagement did not proceed to marriage."

"I repeat my apology. I accept I cannot make amends and that there is no prospect of repairing our relationship. I nevertheless hope that you might consider allowing me to purchase Mademoiselle Vauquelin's painting of Honfleur, as a reminder of my misuse of you and of what might have been had I not listened to Monsieur Deveaux."

"You are right. Nothing will ever repair the damage you caused by the rupture of our engagement – the gossip, innuendo and distress to me and my family. Why you should wish to have the painting in your possession, as a reminder of your misuse of me, is frankly beyond my comprehension. I find it bizarre behaviour. But that is of no consequence. The painting is not for sale. Indeed, it will never be. The only act of kindness you can possibly commit is to report Monsieur Deveaux to the police. For what he did was libellous and he should be exposed and punished accordingly. I expect nothing less of you."

With those words, I left the room and returned to Monsieur Tessier, who helped me wrap the paintings and kindly summoned a carriage for me to take them away. That evening I sat in my bedroom, eyes fastened on the face of the woman I had loved, I had kissed and whose body had given me such pleasure. I was overwhelmed, drowning in a sea of grief.

The next morning, I received a letter from Monsieur de Mercier, once again abjectly apologising for his actions and informing me that, the previous afternoon, he had instructed his lawyer to submit a formal request for an investigation into Hector Deveaux's role.

The following days were difficult. While the murder had disappeared from the newspaper headlines, my name and association with Célestine continued to be the subject of gossip. It appeared some of the allegations – all entirely groundless – emanated from sources within the police, acquaintances, it subsequently turned out, of Monsieur Deveaux. My father, urged by my mother, arranged for me to travel to Nevers, in Burgundy, to stay with distant relatives bearing the name Courcel. As the train pulled out of the Gare de l'Est, it was an immense relief to leave Paris behind and in Nevers, my destination, to be able to walk along a street without people pointing fingers at me or whispering behind their hand as I passed.

The evenings, and the nights alone in my bedroom, were hardest for me. In the darkness, I was inconsolable. I found it difficult to sleep and when I did so I had a recurring nightmare – of Célestine dead beside me in bed, her contorted face, those gaping wounds and her eyes, luminous, staring at me. I ate little and spent much time walking alone. The telegram from my father saying that Monsieur Deveaux had been taken from Provence into custody in Paris, for questioning, did little to alleviate my isolation and devastation. There was no one to whom I could disclose my true feelings towards Célestine, no one to whom I could entrust my secret.

A week later my father telegraphed again to say that, following further police enquiries, an examining magistrate had been appointed to conduct formal investigations not only into Célestine's murder but also into related matters involving others who would now be required to give testimony prior to likely prosecution. Though he assured me that I was not suspected of any criminal involvement, it would be necessary for me to return to Paris to provide my own testimony. The thought of returning to Paris filled me with great foreboding. To assist me, my great-uncle Gilbert arranged for me to meet a young lawyer, Charles de Chastain, who served the interests of the Courcel family, as his father had done, with distinction, over many years.

With misgivings, but anxious to dispel any unfounded allegations that might still be levelled against me, I accompanied my uncle to Maître de Chastain's chambers. Though young he was confident in manner, and though unsmiling was immediately sympathetic and understanding. Having sought my uncle's permission for us to speak alone, he asked me what I would wish to make clear to the examining magistrate and what I would like him, as the lawyer representing me, to argue in any criminal proceedings that might ensue from the examining magistrate's conclusions. He said it was essential that I was truthful in what I told him, that I should withhold no information, however private, which, if revealed by others, might cast me in a poor light. It was necessary to show I had nothing to hide. While I might find this difficult, I should be brave and bear with pride the name Courcel – a family name dating back to the early fifteenth century in the ancient Burgundian dukedom. Taking occasional notes, he listened without interruption to my story, exactly as I have told it to you, including the closeness of my friendship with Célestine. It was hard then, as it has been now, to lay bare the most intimate details of our cherished friendship.

When I had finished, and after asking several questions for factual clarification, Maître de Chastain said he accepted what I had told him without qualification or doubt in his mind. He was convinced I had told him the truth and he would confidently draw on my testimony as necessary in any trial resulting from the examining magistrate's findings. He promised, as my representative, to do whatever was necessary to protect my name and to defend my spotless character and the honour of my family. I felt at last that a heavy yoke had been lifted from my shoulders. I was effusive in my gratitude.

"Maître de Chastain, I thank you for your kindness, your patience and for your belief in me. I wish to accept your offer to advise me on my return to Paris to answer questions from the examining magistrate and to present my evidence in any criminal prosecution that might follow. I am entirely blameless in this matter but have suffered grievously from the loss of Mademoiselle Vauquelin whom I truly loved, with the same intimacy and completeness as between a woman and a man – and perhaps more. My relationship with her may cause others profound disquiet and offend their morals but I consider such opinions immaterial to what is to be decided. Though I hope her murderer will be found and punished, any satisfaction I may feel will never repair my loss."

"Mademoiselle Courcel, I understand better than others your position, your inclinations and your suffering. Most of all, however, I have abundant admiration for your bravery and nobility."

I returned home with my uncle. After a further brief meeting, Maître de Chastain and I began our journey to Paris and my appearance before you. There is nothing further for me to tell you. I have told you everything.

* * * * *

The examining magistrate put down his pen and removing his pince-nez looked directly at Anne-Sophie Courcel.

"Thank you, mademoiselle, for your testimony, delivered with clarity, poise and openness. I have one last question. Have you at any time ever had contact of any description, direct or indirect, with either Monsieur Deveaux or Monsieur de Beaudreau or, for that matter, Madame de Beaudreau? Have they ever spoken to you or sought to do so?"

"No contact whatsoever. Nor has my family," she replied with evident disdain.

"Thank you, mademoiselle, I have no further questions. Your involvement with these proceedings is at an end. I have already received formal notice that Maître de Chastain will represent you in court should that eventuality arise – but purely as a possible witness, I must emphasise, and nothing more."

PART THREE

The Reckoning

CHAPTER FOURTEEN

The Examining Magistrate

It has been written in my lifetime that no human authority – neither the King nor the Minister of Justice nor indeed the Prime Minister – can intrude on the power of the *juge d'instruction*, no one can stop him, no one give him orders. He is sovereign, obeying only his conscience and the law.

I agree with those words of Monsieur de Balzac. As I sit at my desk in the spring of 1878, I am supreme. In my hands, in what I write and utter, I hold the fate of others. But that mantle of supremacy brings an all-too-human burden: the frequent struggle of conscience and application of the law versus pusillanimity – on the latter side the temptation to ignore the legal merits, the strength of the evidence gathered, what I know and feel to be right, and to conclude instead that a case should not go to trial, with the self-serving intention to win praise from those who would prefer their malign interests to remain undisturbed. At the request of the *procureur*, I ordered the investigation, issued search warrants and compelled the witnesses in this drama to appear to give evidence or to submit written testimony. In some instances, the witnesses heard each other's testimony. Now I must decide whether to issue an order of *non-lieu* – no case – or commit the case to the trial court. If I decide the latter, the Chamber of Accusation of the Court of Appeal may still reject my recommendation, but the teeth of the judicial machinery will already have begun to bite and grind. The lives of these *dramatis personae* will never be the same. What happens will hinge on my written decision. It will not be an easy one to reach.

This case brings face to face two other powerful forces in this city. The first is wealth, represented by two rich and influential families, scions of the haute bourgeoisie that dominate Paris in our 6th, 8th and 16th arrondissements. One of those families embodies the limitless acquisition of money through commercial enterprise, the other the exercise of silky persuasion through charismatic legal advocacy, the enhancement of reputation through winning cases. The matching force of strength, with its own interests to defend and axes to grind, is the police – powerful, frequently unchecked, determined. In between these two opposing goliaths is a family more modest in means, influence and renown – but bearing an ancient Burgundian name. Holding the ring is me, the *juge d'instruction*. Everyone awaits my verdict. That fills me with pride, further inflating, I must admit, my sense of self-importance. When it becomes too manifest, my wife, Madame Levasseur, reminds me yet again of the Bible's warning that pride goes before destruction and a haughty spirit before a fall.

So, the time has come for me – and me alone – to decide what should happen in this case. I have read carefully the written testimony and listened attentively to the oral statements. Everybody awaits my words. In the past I have been untroubled by the difficult cases I've investigated. Indeed, I have relished them as opportunities to burnish my reputation. But this case of murder causes me unease and I must tread with caution as I consider my decision.

Of course, giving in to temptation, with its lure of even higher legal office, is one option, the easy one. I could sweep every fact aside and conclude that no further action should be taken, allow the de Beaudreau and d'Aurevalle families to go on their way with unblemished character – dismiss their actions as the frivolous self-indulgent fancies of the powerful. After all, even my head is sometimes turned by a beautiful young woman and thoughts of what a liaison with her would be like. The Courcel family would not, of course, benefit from such a judgement. They would remain grievously affronted by the treatment of their blameless daughter and the loss of her companion in tragic circumstances. Yet that would weigh little against ensuring the continuing interests of two families, pillars of Parc Monceau society, resting easily in their luxurious town houses. The French state has undergone so many convulsions within the past century. Why put much-valued and esteemed bourgeois stability at risk?

And what of the police, embodied in this case by Monsieur Deveaux? They are part of the essential glue that holds our society together. As an important arm of the French state, surely they should have the freedom to pursue their work as they think best, without challenge, using their judgement as to the methods they should employ. Mistakes may have been made in this case but why should the conduct of a former police officer with an ailing wife tarnish the force's reputation? Nor must I overlook the fact that I depend on them for the conduct of investigations, to carry out my instructions, to bring me what I require. Their contribution underpins my present reputation as an honourable examining magistrate.

In these circumstances, I could easily turn a blind legal eye. Indeed, I am already being urged by some around me that it would be best to let sleeping dogs lie. Such passivity on my part would, I am confident, lead to further public recognition – not least in the Ministry of Justice and the presidential palace – of my wisdom in determining when a case should go no further. After all, I began my career in the south-west, far removed from Paris, but through the acquisition of influential patrons I now sit as one of the most eminent and respected *juges d'instruction* in the French capital, tipped, my informers tell me, for higher office, as someone who in delicate cases can be relied upon to reach sensible, balanced conclusions. And such an outcome would greatly please Madame Levasseur, my wife. She too has her eyes on a town house in the vicinity of the Parc Monceau. To do nothing, therefore, would be so easy, so praiseworthy in the minds of those who matter and so rewarding for my future prospects. To do the opposite – to order a trial – would be more problematic, make a stir, be grist to the newspapers' mill, cause embarrassment to the families involved, provoke anger among the police, so defensive of their members and methods. As you can see, it is a hard decision I have to make: let sleeping dogs lie or goad the powerful. The temptation of the easy option is a worthy opponent of my conscience.

Let me consider the circumstances once more.

Émile de Beaudreau and his wife, Monique, the much-loved daughter of Gabriel d'Aurevalle, were, socially, a widely celebrated couple. Together they had great wealth, style and influence and, adding to the spice, she is a great beauty, lionised by the haute bourgeoisie and often the subject of newspaper gossip; the soirées she has graced are almost legendary. The utter disregard of each for others, their self-absorption and supreme vanity blinded them to their inner fragility in the hands of capricious Fortune, who, being both devil and ministering angel, bestows gifts but snatches them away at whim.

This case is about a flaw in the character of an individual determined to stop at nothing to satisfy his egoistic appetite, even to the point of intervening to stop the marriage of two young people he did not know. Yet we all have weaknesses and secrets, troubling inclinations and fantasies. I too, an eminent examining magistrate, have secrets I would not wish others to know. Yes. It would be so easy to conclude that no crime had been committed, the only guilt self-delusions that got out of hand and limitless disregard for others, the only offence that of greed for money, with the unintended consequence of tragic loss of life. Surely that would be the best conclusion, a right and proper one. I could then attend to other matters.

Yet my conscience stops me. Mademoiselle Courcel, whose testimony and demeanour were so compelling, contrasts sharply with the self-serving machinations of two families shielded by their wealth, pride and contempt for others. Should she be sacrificed in a judgement of no action taken to avoid a decision that goes against established interests? It was Brutus in Shakespeare's play *Julius Caesar* who uttered the words, "Th' abuse of greatness is when it disjoins remorse from power". Should I close my eyes and be merciful to wealth and power, though they themselves have abused their position in showing neither pity nor repentance, or should I meet the unbending standards of the law and thus avoid my conscience forever damning me as a hypocrite? And then there is the great Molière to consider. No shirker of ridiculing the powerful, he wrote: "It is not only for what we do that we are held responsible, but also for what we do not do." If I am to follow his advice, I must resist a rush to judgement and look dispassionately at the facts.

The instigator of these events is Émile de Beaudreau. This man of strong intellect and equal vanity had everything he could possibly want – a famous and respected family name, wealth, influence and the prospect of a career likely to have given him even greater prominence and respect. Moreover, he had married a beautiful woman, daughter of one of the richest men in Paris. Together they had the promise of a life of luxury and influence. But he had a disturbing flaw in his character. He believed that whatever he desired was his for the taking, whether it be art or women, regardless of the cost and regardless of what others might think. He was impervious to those around him.

It was he who, according to his written admission, set in motion a train of events that was to have tragic consequences. Like a child coveting a toy, he desired on mere impulse that Mademoiselle Courcel, whom he had never met, only seen, should be his. His impulse became an obsession. He spent huge sums of money in its pursuit, his efforts to possess her undermining his fortune as well as his sanity. He would stop at nothing to manipulate her future in order to achieve his end: this beautiful young woman in his bed and no one else's. As *Le Petit Journal* put it, in one of its pithy reports, he squandered it all. All he gained from the fortune he spent were two paintings of Mademoiselle Courcel, secured for him at the cost of three lives; two paintings which he hung in his villa to gaze at for hours on end, pretending they were together in bed.

A greater sin was to betray his country by passing confidential government information to a woman who, together with her master, regarded France as their enemy, and who were intent on thwarting the Republic's imperial ambitions to protect their own. A victim of her oriental wiles, de Beaudreau surrendered to blackmail in order to avoid the revelation of his obsession. What he did was shameful and traitorous. It was another manifestation of his weakness and his failure to escape the ever-tightening grip of his obsession.

Yet arguably his greatest sin was to covet a young woman to such an extent that he engineered the termination of her engagement, altering her life, her family's and that of Monsieur Alexandre de Mercier, and indirectly brought about the death of her close companion, Mademoiselle Vauquelin.

I had many questions to put to him but that was not to be. He committed suicide in his villa in Provence. Sitting in a chair, facing the two paintings of Mademoiselle Courcel, this man of unparalleled arrogance and self-deceit shot himself in the head, according to the local police. The extent of his culpability, the part he played in this case, is set out in the meticulous notes he made of his correspondence with Monsieur Deveaux and his detailed record of the sums of money he paid to the former detective. These notes, which he stored in a wooden chest in the cellar first of the Hue residence and then of the villa in Provence, are at present in my possession and I will decide in due course whether to release them to the family or to retain them in my keeping for the foreseeable future.

Monsieur de Beaudreau's actions were despicable but I suspect not uncommon amongst the haute bourgeoisie.

Monique de Beaudreau is a beautiful, ambitious, articulate, possessive and manipulative woman. She follows in the footsteps of her late father.

Together they plotted her marriage to Émile de Beaudreau. In the mind of Gabriel d'Aurevalle, it was the ultimate match – the coming together of two dynasties from a social tier forever aspiring to higher, greater, more. For him it was akin to a royal marriage alliance. The benefits would be endless. But Monsieur d'Aurevalle had secrets. Ambitious entrepreneurs tread on people who get in their way, sometimes in a vicious manner. The police were aware of some of the things he did, but chose not to intervene. After all, if they needed information from time to time, they knew who to turn to, who might give them interesting facts. If he helped them, they would turn a blind eye to his methods. How do I know this? Because my allies, the police, have told me.

His daughter, Monique, behaved similarly in the way she used money and lies to court admiration and praise, to get what she wanted. She had numerous affairs, to which she alluded in her

testimony. Her fascination with the illicit, her attraction to its excitement, brought her to the attention of Madame de Cassin. Madame de Beaudreau has related what she did one evening at the de Cassin residence. She claimed that only once did she perform the role of a prostitute. But that is not true. She provided such services more than once, enjoyed doing so and relished the thrill of receiving payment. I have uncovered this fact from a witness in the de Cassin household, who I will come to in a moment.

Once his daughter's marriage to Émile de Beaudreau became a distinct possibility, to ensure that her relationship with Madame de Cassin – and perhaps also his own – remained a secret and did not jeopardise the alliance, Gabriel d'Aurevalle made two substantial payments: one to secure Madame de Cassin's silence and another, through an intermediary, to Chief Inspector Deveaux. The purpose of the latter payment was to remove from Paris the presence of another prostitute – the masked woman, Suzanne, whom Monique d'Aurevalle had met on the first occasion she performed. It was Suzanne who had written the anonymous letter to her some time later, demanding money after she had been dismissed from Madame de Cassin's ménage. What's more, the threads in this web of frailty and deceit being more tightly interwoven than many of its victims – or spinners – could have guessed, she was the aunt of the Emperor's concubine. Removal meant her death in a street "accident": she was run over by a horse and carriage.

Madame de Beaudreau's discovery, after arriving in Hue, that her husband was apparently in correspondence with Monsieur Deveaux, caused her great alarm. She wrote to her father to alert him, fearful of the exposure of her secret and the risk it would pose to her marriage. Together, they decided to tread with care in case the correspondence was unconnected. After a while, as de Beaudreau had not accused his wife of concealing facts that might have rendered good grounds for declaring their union null and void, they concluded that it was safe to let the matter rest rather than make discreet enquiries in Paris. As we know from Monsieur de Beaudreau's written testimony, that was in fact the case. He did not know that his wife had performed as a prostitute. He was in touch with Monsieur Deveaux solely to pursue his obsession with Mademoiselle Courcel.

Monique de Beaudreau did not escape the attention of Mademoiselle Nguyen Thi Phuong, who had been educated in Paris and was cared for, during that time, by her aunt. The mademoiselle's written testimony – and indeed that of the Emperor – revealed Monique de Beaudreau's indiscreet disclosures to her and the skilful and damaging use to which she put them – namely to blackmail Émile de Beaudreau. But Mademoiselle Nguyen also soon recognised the d'Aurevalle family's connection with her aunt. She decided that not only would she blackmail Émile de Beaudreau, she would also compromise his wife, by involving her in an affair with Pham Thanh Quoc. In due course that might furnish an opportunity to destroy the de Beaudreau marriage and thus wreak partial revenge for what had happened to her aunt.

In her testimony to me, Madame de Beaudreau wore a mask of near inscrutability. Behind it lay deep emotions, stirred by what has happened to her. Yet, despite it all, she remains a woman of iron, determined to cast off the memory of her husband and devote herself to the advancement of her father's enterprises – unless I decide that the case should go to trial, in which case her persona will be exposed for what it is worth.

As for the Emperor and his concubine, there is much I could say but I know from the private message I received recently from the Ministry of Foreign Affairs that it is the Minister's explicit wish that what happened in Hue should be regarded as confidential and be left unstated, in the interest of the security of the French state and its longer-term ambitions in Cochinchina and the surrounding territories – and, of course, to avoid public embarrassment. I have no wish to go against his wishes.

I understand Monsieur Fournier will shortly be replaced as Resident Superior, at the end of his extended period of office, retiring immediately afterwards with suitable public recognition. Lieutenant Tihon has been exonerated in all respects, promoted and returned to his unit.

*

Chief Inspector Deveaux was a pillar of the Paris police force during his long career. Many have communicated privately to me their accounts of his steadfast sense of duty, in particular his skill, foresight and determination during periods of civic unrest. His personal views about the behaviour of the haute bourgeoisie and his antipathy towards them were not widely known, confined to his close colleagues, many of whom were of the same opinion.

In his testimony, he hid no details. He told the full truth, no matter how unpalatable. Motivated by his dislike of what Émile de Beaudreau represented and concerned about the increasing cost of caring for his ailing wife, he saw the opportunity to earn money. Monsieur de Beaudreau's readiness to pay, without any obvious limit, for the pursuit of his obsession turned the head of the former chief inspector. He became a victim of greed, earning and desiring ever greater sums. Whatever he charged, his client paid – through the nose. As a senior policeman, Deveaux had always been well aware of the risks of overstepping the mark, pushing the boundaries too far in any enterprise. He had always exercised admirable caution in order to avoid overexposure in his campaign against the opponents of the police. But the ease with which his demands for ever increasing sums of money were met by his client rapidly caused him to become careless, to ignore the risks he was taking. Soon, he lost all sense of proportion, before long gaining an increasing thrill from what he was doing. Killing two women in Seville may have caused him some temporary distress but it did not unnerve him. Callously, he regarded them as casualties of war. They had simply got in the way of a defensible objective, pursued on behalf of his client. He returned to Paris with the painting he had stolen, almost proud of what he had done. That theft and the earlier one from the rue Frochot were trophies attesting to his skill.

The letter from Mademoiselle Vauquelin, however, did unnerve him. If he failed to stop her, the edifice he had created could come crashing to the ground. He claimed he tried to reason with her but that she was uncompromising in her demands. In his effort to subdue her, he grabbed the knife she was holding and she died, stabbed in the neck. Whether or not her killing was premeditated, it was disastrous.

Yet again, he showed little remorse but realised that the relationship with his client had to end. He had already accumulated a substantial amount of money, far more than he had ever imagined. He and his increasingly frail wife could finally leave polluted eastern Paris and move to Provence. But his now ingrained greed caused him to gamble for one last time.

While the former detective knew as much about his client as his client knew about him, it was necessary to take one final step. When the two met, he agreed to the proposal to surrender his own records of all that had happened between them, but only if Monsieur de Beaudreau agreed to purchase for him and his wife the neighbouring villa Maison de Dieu. This was an ambitious proposition, which would cement the Faustian pact between them. They would be bound together for the foreseeable future, constantly reminded of what they knew about each other. Moreover, with the house purchased for him, Monsieur Deveaux would retain a considerable amount of unspent money. And so it came about. But with the death of Émile de Beaudreau this precarious idyll crumbled, leading to my instruction to the police to bring Monsieur Deveaux to Paris and place him in custody. Following her husband's removal from Provence, Madame Deveaux died. Maison de Dieu remains unoccupied, as does the de Beaudreau summer villa – both memorials to the dangerous paths of obsession and greed.

And what should I say of Mademoiselle Courcel?

An arrestingly beautiful young woman, quietly spoken, poised and graceful, her testimony was moving. It is evident to me that she is entirely blameless in this sad affair. That fateful day on the river the mademoiselle was unaware she and her companion, rapt in each other and the sonnets of Shakespeare, had triggered events that would end in death and disgrace for two powerful families, the downfall of a respected police officer, three murders and the loss of her beloved cousin. The treatment she and her equally innocent family have received in recent weeks from the newspapers has been lamentable to say the least. She deserved far greater comfort, understanding and privacy. The nature of the relationship between her and Mademoiselle

Vauquelin may be of interest to the prurient but it has no bearing on this matter. Whatever my decision, I must do all that I can to protect her from unnecessary further exposure.

That is the cast of characters before me. But I had almost forgotten — there was one testimony I was unable to hear and evaluate, despite several requests to the military authorities: that of Lieutenant Tihon, who, I have heard recently, has been rapidly promoted, leapfrogging the rank of captain to that of lieutenant-colonel, in recognition of exemplary service to the state. The reason for such a step has not been disclosed — not even to me — but I must say I find it surprising, given that he broke the strict rules of the French mission in Hue by allowing Monsieur de Beaudreau to remove a confidential diplomatic codebook from official premises and, compounding the dereliction, did not insist on its immediate return. His action led to the compromise of communications with the Ministry in Paris. He was summoned back to France for examination by the military, with the likely prospect of serious punishment. From his letter to Monsieur de Beaudreau, it was evident he was going to lay all the blame at the door of the Deputy Resident Superior in order to seek mitigation. But a short while later he was exonerated and subsequently promoted two ranks. What service did he perform to earn this exceptional accolade? I am tempted to hazard a guess as to what he might have done — or been obliged to do — but will resist and not speculate further since it has been made clear to me within the Palais de Justice that the officer and his part in this case are beyond my civilian legal remit.

So, those are the facts that emerged from what I have heard and read. All the ingredients of this sad and tawdry case are on the table. Everyone's deeds, interests and motivations have been exposed, except, of course, the Lieutenant's. He to one side, everybody, apart from Mademoiselle Courcel, appears in a poor light — their actions, their behaviour, all motivated by the baser traits of human nature. What should be the cost? Who should pay the price for the shedding of blood, the betrayal of France? Questions it is up to me to answer.

Shortly, I must complete my written decision.

CHAPTER FIFTEEN

The Decision

That evening I still wrestled with my conscience. What was right and what would be wrong? No case had so troubled my legal mind. As I dined with my wife and some of her friends, only half listening to conversations on matters of utter irrelevance to me, I still could not decide what my verdict should be. My failure to make up my mind, my indecisiveness, greatly irritated me. This had never happened before. I had always been confident, certain; now I was perplexed. I tried to understand what exactly the impediment was. Was it genuine doubt? Or an inclination to procrastinate, to put off a decision on account of intellectual laziness towards writing a convincing judgement, pulling all the threads together? Or was it simply manifest lack of courage?

In bed, unable to sleep, I asked myself the same question over and over again. Should I, as a respected examining magistrate, follow my conscience and the strict application of the law on the basis of compelling testimony and evidence, and thus send Hector Deveaux, currently in La Santé prison, to trial? After all, he and the late unlamented Émile de Beaudreau were instigators of events that had swept others along like flotsam on a raging river to a dark vortex from which there had been no escape. Of course, to commit the former police inspector to trial would expose to public ridicule and condemnation what lay beneath the upturned stone. Reputations would be irrevocably damaged. On the other hand, I could choose to heap all blame on Émile de Beaudreau, no longer able to defend his name, and order the release of Hector Deveaux, permitting him to sink into obscurity in his river-bank house. The two illustrious families – what was left of them – could go about their business in the safe expectation that the affair would soon be forgotten, just as a sandcastle is washed away by the incoming tide, no trace of it remaining as the water ebbs. It should have been so easy to decide on the basis of fact and yet I still found cause to vacillate. In short, I stood at a fork in the road but rooted to the spot, unable to choose which path to take, to put one foot before the other. Conscience and Weakness stood shoulder to shoulder beneath the signpost, each urging me in their direction.

The following day, at breakfast, my wife asked if I had decided what to do. I replied that I could not discuss with her the case or my conclusions. She countered it was evident to her that I remained undecided and my indecision was, she said, uncharacteristic. I did not respond.

Later in the day, I went to my chambers in the annex to the Palais de Justice – close to Notre-Dame, the Sainte-Chapelle and the Conciergerie, made infamous by the Revolution – to inform my clerks that I would deliver my verdict at noon the following day. I gave instructions that the police should bring Hector Deveaux from prison to the building, in case his presence should be necessary. My clerks asked what conclusion I had reached. I told them they would know soon enough. After writing some notes about what I might say and locking them in my safe, to which only I had access, I went for a walk in the Jardin du Luxembourg in the 6th arrondissement of Paris – the heart of the city's wealth.

I often walk alone in the park to clear my head before a judgement, to put the issues of a case into sharper perspective. If fresh thoughts occur to me, I jot them down immediately in a small notebook I carry with me at all times so that whatever crosses my mind will not be lost. For that case more than any other, I had to be alone.

It was a pleasant spring day, the much cared for park in fine seasonal shape. In the calm atmosphere, I followed the terrace past the statues, including the queens of France – such as Marguerite of Navarre, Blanche of Castile, Margaret of Provence – pondering on their role in the nation's history. I walked on to reach my favourite spot: the Medici Fountain, built by the widow of King Henry IV and regent of King Louis XIII. Now restored after the tribulations of the Revolution and settled in its new position, its long basin of water reflected the plane trees that flanked it on either side. Here I lingered for a while, acutely aware – as a distant bell struck the hour – that tomorrow I and no one else would finally deliver the verdict: to release Hector Deveaux or have him sent back to La Santé to await trial. Once more everyone, everything, would hang on my unchallengeable words. What power we examining magistrates possess!

Leaving the park, I passed some of the grand town houses of the rich and powerful. Several times in recent years my wife had expressed the wish that perhaps the time would come when I would be sufficiently famous and well-heeled for us to live there. I too shared that ambition. I knew my decision the next day would bring that nearer or make it more remote.

That evening my senior clerk delivered an urgent and confidential message from the governor of La Santé prison. Hector Deveaux, while in the custody to which I had consigned him, had been found dead in his cell. The cause of death had not yet been established. The clerk asked if I wished to proceed as planned at noon the following day. I replied without hesitation that I did. Despite that act of bravado, I went to bed deeply troubled. The two principal instigators of the affair I had been investigating were now both dead. Was it pure coincidence or were darker forces – forces of the French state – at play? An inquiry into his death was necessary and had already commenced. But it was an inquiry conducted by the police concerning the death of a former and much respected colleague. I wondered whether they would be truly honest and impartial in the conclusions they drew from whatever evidence might be available to them or whether this would be a convenient opportunity to claim they had drawn a blank.

The following morning, I went early to the judicial building, unsure how best to proceed in the circumstances that had arisen so unexpectedly. A small crowd had gathered outside and two or three newspaper reporters were present. I had barely taken off my coat and settled at my desk to write my conclusion when the door opened. A tall, lean-faced man with oil-darkened hair entered unannounced, one of my clerks trying to pull him back.

"Let him enter. I was expecting him."

I beckoned my visitor to sit in front of the desk. He did so. There was something unpleasant, even menacing about him.

"I'm here on behalf of the Minister of Justice. He wishes to know, in the light of Monsieur Deveaux's untimely death, what you intend to conclude in your statement later this morning."

Now, finally, was the moment to reveal my decision – the triumph of conscience and legal application over pusillanimity.

"I intend to say that, had he lived, I would have sent Monsieur Deveaux for trial for the murder of Mademoiselle Vauquelin. I will add that over the past weeks I have given this matter intense thought, that I have listened with great attention to his testimony and that of others, and that I have painstakingly examined the compelling evidence in my possession. I have concluded that this is a case where due process should apply, despite the status and the recent fate of those involved."

I sat back. My interlocutor gazed at me intently.

"The Minister has instructed me to convey to you that your decision today should be cancelled."

"Why is the Minister of that opinion?"

"It is not for me to say," my visitor replied curtly.

This man was irritating me more than ever.

"I need hardly remind you that as a *juge d'instruction*, under the law of this country I am independent of political pressure, which is what I consider is being applied here. It is for me and me alone to decide how to proceed, not the Minister or his superior, the Prime Minister, or even the President."

"That may be your view –"

I interrupted.

"It is not my view. It is the law."

"That may be your interpretation," he continued, "but it remains the Minister's strong wish – instruction, if I may put it another way – that your verdict should be adjourned *sine die* without any pronouncement on your part."

"And if I choose to ignore the Minister and proceed?"

I knew already what he would say. My antagonist in this conversation oozed the very power and corruption that Hector Deveaux had witnessed and abhorred as a police officer. There was the stink of the devil about this Ministerial messenger. Perhaps he *was* the devil – come to challenge what my conscience had guided me to do after so much mental anguish.

"It may adversely affect your esteemed reputation and, moreover, your future prospects. It is the Minister's opinion that, as an examining magistrate, you are already greatly respected for your wisdom, perspicacity and legal efficaciousness. Why undermine that by not following his advice? He believes there is much more you can achieve in your remaining career. But in this particular matter he urges you to defer to his wishes."

"I suppose influence, money and power have intervened," I remarked, my resignation not without anger. "It is hard for me to judge whether they are being applied by those who live in the 6th and 16th arrondissements of this city or by the Minister of the Interior."

"Sir, let us not debate how many angels can dance on the head of a pin. Such pedantry is out of place in this affair. It is simply a delicate matter that has to be resolved, quietly and expediently. That is what the Minister requires."

"And what about Mademoiselle Courcel and her murdered cousin? What comfort can they find in the Minister's 'wishes', as you euphemistically describe them? Does he have no regard for the three principles of the Revolution. I need hardly remind you what they are – liberty, equality and fraternity. What the Minister is effectively ordering me to do offers the Courcel family no equality before the law."

"That is not a subject on which I can comment. I was asked to convey a clear instruction and I have done so. Now I seek your reply, which the Minister urgently awaits."

We looked at each other, two swordsmen, epées ready to strike.

Neither he nor I spoke, the only sound the ticking of the clock on the table across from my desk and the pit-pat of rain against the window. Once again I faced a testing choice: either to comply, and so compromise my principles, or to disregard the instruction and proceed with a verdict that would inevitably be ignored.

I muttered out loud the remark attributed to Louis XV after the Battle of Rossbach in 1757: "*Après moi, le deluge.*"

"It is for you to decide whether to drown in the consequences of your obstinacy," my interlocutor countered.

I rang the bell on my desk. The clerk entered.

"Today's verdict is adjourned. There will be no conclusion. Please convey that message to those waiting outside."

"Is there a new date?" the clerk asked.

"No. The adjournment is *sine die.*"

The tall man rose, a smirk on his face.

"I didn't catch your name."

"My name is irrelevant. Suffice it to say the Minister will be pleased with your wise decision. I imagine your wisdom will be repaid with public recognition before long."

"Will it be the Minister who is pleased or will it be others who secured his connivance?"

He did not reply. Smiling, he put on his hat and closed the door behind him.

Before the Minister's agents descended to ensure I did not change my mind, I quickly gathered together on my desk the full dossier of evidence and testimony. Flicking through the sheaves of documents, I passed to my senior clerk all the papers I considered redundant, of no further use and therefore suitable for destruction. I had to throw the wolves some meat. I instructed him to place them in the vault with the chest containing Émile de Beaudreau's meticulous record of his correspondence with Hector Deveaux; I knew they would be collected soon by the appropriate authority in the Palais de Justice. While the clerks did as I asked, alone in my office I bound with blue ribbon a separate file in which I had placed my personal notes on the testimony given to me, including my copy of Émile de Beaudreau's written

confession, found beside his body and sent to me by the police in Provence. I put the file in my leather briefcase. On my senior clerk's return, I asked him to bring me the papers relating to my next case. I would begin my examination of the facts the following week. Within an hour or so, all trace of the affair had been removed from my office.

As I left the building by a rear entrance, I witnessed, as anticipated, the arrival of officials from the Palais de Justice to remove the chest containing the de Beaudreau papers. I had little doubt they would soon be disposed of, together with my own documents. Destruction would be swift. After all, in any wrongdoing, all incriminating evidence should rapidly vanish to facilitate plausible deniability. Instead of going home immediately, I took a cab to visit – via a circuitous route – my patiently waiting *amoureuse*. I looked forward to her embrace and physical comfort. After an aperitif and other pleasures, I departed leaving the precious file well hidden in her safe care. If I did not soon receive the recognition I had been promised, I would have the means to press my case – should I wish to use that weapon, double-edged though it might prove.

Later that evening, after my wife and I had dined and she had gone to bed, I began to write this brief account of the circumstances surrounding the conclusion – or rather, indefinite suspension – of this case. Almost ready to put down my pen, I accept that, in the end, despite my espousal and indeed vigorous articulation of noble principles, I have been pusillanimous, a hypocrite. I gave in, compromised those principles and my conscience, under pressure to comply with the wishes of the Minister, who himself had clearly been under great political pressure. In compromising, I have also failed Mademoiselle Courcel. While she can justly consider herself cheated of justice, I, on account of what I have done, will be rewarded with further promotion and Madame Levasseur will be a step nearer the Parc Monceau.

CHAPTER SIXTEEN

A Character in Someone Else's Story

It is 1879. More than a year has elapsed since my lawyer, Maître Charles de Chastain, informed me that the distinguished *juge d'instruction*, Monsieur Levasseur, had adjourned *sine die* the sitting at which he was due to deliver his decision on whether the former detective, Hector Deveaux, should be sent for trial for the murder of my cousin, Célestine Vauquelin.

Because of Émile de Beaudreau's capricious but fast-rooted fancy one Sunday afternoon four years ago and his subsequent devilish pact with Deveaux, I lost Célestine. I still grieve for her, for missed love, missed opportunities. It's a wound I fear will never heal. The perpetrators of this heinous crime paid a heavy price for their self-indulgence and greed, but while they are gone, I bear the life-long scars.

Unlike Célestine, I am not a painter. I have rich images in my mind and am much drawn to painting, but however hard I try I cannot transmit to canvas in eloquent brush strokes what I imagine and see around me. If anything, I am a writer. Since I was young I have kept a diary – at first a simple daily record of things done and people met. As I grew older, the diaries became more a record of thoughts and feelings. The journals of my time with Célestine are intense and intimate, often written in highly charged and overwrought prose. I open them sometimes to relive those interludes of blissful happiness, particularly that magical summer in Provence. I still keep a diary. To write – often quite long passages – gives me freedom of expression, rising above social constraints and the chaos of this world. When Célestine and I had become lovers, I thought of perhaps writing a book about love between two women. What I would write she would illustrate, express in paint – the emotion, the physical closeness and the happiness I imagined would be ours. It was unlikely the book would ever be published – except one or two copies printed for our personal possession – but for us it would be a testament of our profound love for one another. And then she was taken from me.

Though Célestine is gone, my writing enables me to represent myself as I am. As no one sees what I write, I can take liberties with forms and structures, with people, places, oceans, clouds. I am mistress of all I survey, all that I think and all that I do. One day, when I am dead, perhaps what I have written will become known. Readers will either be scandalised or deeply touched by what they see of me, at ease in an intensely private realm. After Célestine's death I still wrote but found it hard to put the words onto the paper, so desolate was I, though I did my best to mask my grief in the company of others. But as the months passed, the words began to flow once more, despite my sadness. I do not know why it should have been so but I felt liberated – not, of course, from the precious recollections of my lover but from self-imposed inhibition.

Memories became vivid again, much sharper than before. Célestine, Provence and Seville resurfaced, more vibrant and less painful, the emotion better expressed as I wrote each page. I thrive when I am alone in my simply furnished writing room, surrounded by Célestine's presence – including her self-portrait, her paintings of me in Provence and Seville and the Honfleur beachscape that I had refused to let Alexandre de Mercier have. I regarded it after her death as my studio, where I could paint pictures in words; I still do. The isolation of this room over the past months has never distressed me, far from it. If what I write secluded from the world is ever published, I would like my words to speak to other young women who may have suffered the fate I endured. Since the termination of the examining magistrate's proceedings, my supreme challenge has been to break free from being a character in the story of Émile de Beaudreau's obsession and become the principal character in my own – to find a role entirely disconnected from his, with the eventual consequence that he will be entirely forgotten while I will be remembered as a writer of honesty and intimacy, creating pictures with words.

Venturing back into the world after Célestine's death, I have met many people, had my hand kissed by young men seeking my attention, been urged by my mother to fall in love and travelled frequently to Spain, to dwell once more on the sights, sounds and smells of Andalucía. Though my parents have longed for me to marry, I have so far resisted. I have found no woman in friendship to match my cousin in temperament or attraction and no man with whom I have had the desire to share physical intimacy. For all my efforts, though more than a year has elapsed since it all ended, I still observe occasional finger-pointing in the street and hear those who whisper behind their hand: "There goes the de Beaudreau woman." So far, I'm still a character in his story. But there is one event in recent times that has helped me to flourish, to find even greater self-expression in my writing and finally to begin to secure separation from the past. It is my correspondence with Maître de Chastain. I look often at what he wrote – how it all began.

It started with his unexpected letter to me after his return to Nevers in 1878, following the abandonment of the magistrate's verdict. Before he left Paris, I had thanked him for the great kindness and understanding he had shown me. His goodbye had been courteous though somewhat perfunctory, which I subsequently put down to shyness. Almost a month had passed before his letter arrived. I read it carefully. Should I reply or let it be? I decided it would be churlish not to respond.

> *Paris*
> *Monday, the 24th of June 1878*
> *Cher Maître de Chastain,*
> *Thank you for your most considerate letter, sent after your return to Nevers. I much appreciate your kind words.*
> *I express again my regret that your journey to Paris to*

appear on my behalf before the examining magistrate was such a waste of your time when you have so many other more important clients to represent. As you know, Monsieur Levasseur's decision came as a profound disappointment, but in the light of what I have suffered and the loss I have endured nothing surprises me any more.

You may wish to know that my father has engaged a lawyer to ascertain the whereabouts of the two paintings stolen by Monsieur Deveaux – one from Célestine's atelier and the other from the house in which she and I stayed in Seville. I believe they were hanging in Monsieur de Beaudreau's summer villa at the time of his death, but it is conceivable they have been destroyed or are in police custody or that Madame de Beaudreau has had them sold. We will try to find them however long it takes.

I wish you well.
Yours cordially,
Anne-Sophie Courcel

I expected to hear no more but then some three weeks later I received another letter from him, offering, provided my father and I agreed, to represent me in proceedings against Madame de Beaudreau, who, he had established, was now the legal possessor of the paintings, wherever they might be; he was sure they had not been destroyed, at least. His representation would be for a minimum fee.

I consulted my father. We decided we should gladly accept the offer from a much-respected lawyer in Nevers who had served the Courcel family in the Burgundy region and who, moreover, had treated me with great respect and understanding when I went to see him in his chambers. My father wrote to him accordingly but I insisted that I should do so as well.

Paris
Tuesday, the 23rd of July 1878
Dear Maître de Chastain,
Your unexpected letter with its most thoughtful and

generous offer to assist us to recover the two stolen pictures brought us great joy. We accept your generosity, as I am sure you will already know from receipt of my father's letter.

As you might imagine, my disappointment with the examining magistrate's decision remains unassuaged and often transforms into unquenchable anger. I know there is nothing further to be done, as you advised at the time. But the safe return of the two paintings, if, as you indicate, they are indeed still in existence, would bring me at least some personal satisfaction. Possession of them would help to ease my grief and go some way to restore my faith in justice. I note that Monsieur Levasseur has recently been appointed to the Cour de Cassation. I decline to speculate whether this should be viewed as a reward for his previous action!

Yours cordially,

Anne-Sophie Courcel

Some weeks later Maître de Chastain wrote again to say that, as a consequence of urgent correspondence between him and the lawyers acting on behalf of Madame d'Aurevalle, who had reverted to using her father's family name, it had been confirmed that the two paintings still existed and that in principle it was likely I could take possession of them. It would be necessary, however, for me to call on Madame d'Aurevalle at her family home to finalise the matter. On that she was insistent. Because of other legal business he would be unable to accompany me but he had arranged for a trusted friend of his in Versailles, Madame Mareuil, to do so. Unless I met Madame d'Aurevalle in compliance with her wishes – hard though he knew it would be for me to see her – the prospect of reclaiming the paintings would be significantly diminished. Madame Mareuil would make the necessary arrangements on my behalf.

I remember clearly – indeed I will never forget – the day in the autumn of 1878 I went to the d'Aurevalle house. It was on the edge of the Parc Monceau in the 8th arrondissement, a part of the city I seldom had cause to visit. We were shown to the *grand bureau,* luxuriously furnished in the pre-Revolutionary style, the walls draped in richly coloured seventeenth-century tapestries. A few minutes later I was invited to go to the library on the first floor. The room was octagonal in shape; several of the walls were lined with oak bookshelves, each shelf bearing elegant blue- and red-bound volumes. In the middle of the room stood a beautifully carved table with a deep-blue ceramic surface on which sat a gold oriental ornament. Around the table were eight leather-backed chairs each bearing the Bourbon crest. Above the fireplace was a portrait of Gabriel d'Aurevalle. This room and the *grand bureau* bore the sheen of limitless wealth and power, such as one might have seen at Versailles in the reign of Louis XIV. I sat waiting as a loudly ticking clock marked the passing minutes.

A door opened and Madame d'Aurevalle entered. She was taller than I had expected, striking, a formidable, intimidating woman, cold but sexual, who, judging by her manner, was used to getting her way. She sat opposite me, her green eyes fixed on mine, her scornful face framed by waves of long black hair. She uttered no pleasantries.

"I can see how Monsieur de Beaudreau" – she did not refer to him as her late husband – "became obsessed with you, even from a distance. Had he been a painter and you and he had met, you would surely have become his muse and been lured into his bed. But that did not happen. He's gone – my betrayer – and may he suffer in purgatory for his deceit."

"And what of the misery he caused me?" I asked. "The loss of Mademoiselle Vauquelin. Do you not also regret and wish him punished for that?"

"Why should I? You are part of his story, not mine."

"And the paintings stolen by Monsieur Deveaux at your late husband's request – what of those?"

"The paintings you refer to are worthless to me. It is these that have value," she replied, pointing to a large Fragonard and an even larger Boucher on the wall.

"That may be your opinion. But they have personal meaning for me. I should like them returned."

For a moment, she looked away.

"I am told they are at his summer villa. It will shortly be sold but I believe the pictures you seek still hang on the wall where he put them, for the moment. If they are not removed soon, I have no doubt they will be burned."

"Please, Madame d'Aurevalle, do not allow that to happen. Let me have them, I beg you."

Once more she said nothing. The clock measured her silence. Then she reached into her pocket and tossed a small black purse onto the table.

"That is the key to his villa. Take it, go there without delay, remove what you want and leave. As you do so, throw the key into the river."

"Thank you, Madame d'Aurevalle."

She did not reply. Once more, the sound of the ticking clock filled the room.

"I don't think we have anything else to discuss," she said coldly, and with that she rose. "The maid will see you out. You and I will never meet again. Your beauty brought him down. For that I will never forgive you. But you will not also bring me down. To me you mean nothing."

As Madame Mareuil and I left, I looked back towards the house, the embodiment of her late father's success. It was bleak, unloved, a residence of despair and hatred. We walked quickly away.

Less than a week later, Madame Mareuil and I travelled to Provence. Having spent the night at a nearby *relais*, we went to the de Beaudreau summer villa early the next morning, accompanied by a local porter. I unlocked the imposing front door. Inside, I went from room to room, searching for the paintings. Each room was shuttered, thin rays of sunlight penetrating between the cracks, the furniture covered in white shrouds. There was no sign of them. Passing the gilded staircase, I entered a large impressive room with marble pillars in each corner, floor-to-ceiling windows on one side and the unmistakable shape of a piano. At the far end, above a grand ornamental fireplace, was a portrait of Émile de Beaudreau, classical in pose, two large law books on a table beside him. I stood for a moment, confronting my tormentor – for that was what he had been.

Turning, I saw, on the wall opposite the windows, the two pictures: one painted that summer in the house in the woods where Célestine had first made love to me – it felt a lifetime ago and a world away, yet was just across the river – and the other in the house in Seville. Gazing at them, I found it hard to hold back my tears. I pulled the shrouds from the furniture to see where he was said to have sat when he shot himself. Each piece was exquisite in taste. I opened the shutters and, unbolting the central windows, stood in the doorway to the veranda, looking down at the river. This was the view Émile de Beaudreau had of me and Célestine in our boat on that day. Though bathed in the sun's warmth, I felt a deep shiver.

Words – his, not mine – pressed into my head.

"If only this encounter had happened before, it might have been so different – for you and for me. We would have talked, perhaps enjoyed friendship. You would have allowed me to admire your beauty and to show you what might have been – perhaps even persuade you it could still be. How fortune might have smiled on us. Instead, you were a distant, unfulfillable desire that became my obsession. Or was it love? Where does the border between love and obsession lie? All I can claim in my defence is that I was the victim of irresistible attraction, made all the harder to bear because I could never speak to you, touch you. How jealous I was of the inscription on Mademoiselle Vauquelin's portrait of you. She had what I could not.

"In the end, all I could do was run my fingers over your painted image. I became another Tantalus in a Hades of my own construction, surrounded by limitless wealth and pleasure but unable to slake my thirst by having you as mine. Sometimes you were so close, as on that occasion I passed you on the beach. It was as though you were taunting me. Later, when I knew there was no way back from what I had done, I cursed you. But having uttered such shameful words in rage, I then cursed myself for what I had said. You were undeserving of any malediction. I tried to take them back. It was too late. Like the closing chords of a piano sonata, they hung in the air – irretrievable.

"What happened to me should be a warning to others not to cross the boundary between the realm of mortals and the realm of the gods, not to pursue the unattainable. I realised too late I was no god, only a selfish, greedy, flawed mortal. Even now, standing where I once stood, you are no closer, still out of reach as you always were and will forever be."

Anger seethed within me.

"Nothing you may say, nothing you may plead, will ever redeem you. What you could not possess, in vengeance you denied to others. Your actions were vindictive, cruel and destructive. I have no pity for you, nor will I ever have. May you suffer in everlasting purgatory."

"Anne-Sophie, where are you?" I heard a softly spoken voice behind me. "Are you speaking to someone? Who is it? Ah, there you are. I thought you had forgotten me. I think it's time we left."

I spun around to see a shadow advancing across the half-shuttered room. For a moment I stood frozen in fear. Was it him? Was he alive after all?

Out of the gloom stepped Madame Mareuil.

"I'm sure I heard you speaking to someone."

"Only to a ghost of the past," I replied. I pointed to the two paintings. "It's those we should take with us."

She nodded.

"I will ask the porter to take them down and put them in the charabanc. He will arrange for them to be packed, secured and delivered to you in Paris."

"But you are right. It is time we left. I have no wish to stay longer in this mausoleum, home to a dark spirit."

Madame Mareuil replaced the shrouds over the furniture while I shut the windows, slammed home the bolts and closed the shutters. We left the house. As she supervised the porter, I went down the stone steps that led from the veranda to the river bank. I looked at the blue rippling water, its secrets well hidden in its depths. I threw in the key. I turned and as I retraced my steps I looked up at the house for the last time. The shutters of the central window appeared open. I thought I saw a dark-haired man with a handsome saturnine face in a white shirt raise a hand in salutation. I half raised mine in reply. I gasped in horror at what I had done.

"Leave me in peace," I cried, turning away.

When I looked back once more, the shutters were closed as I had left them. There was no figure at the window. It must have been a trick played by my imagination or maybe it was the ghost of Émile de Beaudreau, bidding a last farewell from beyond the grave. Chilled and disturbed, I could not bear to linger a moment longer and ran to the charabanc. When would I ever escape his shadow, his story?

Following my return to Paris, I wrote to Maître de Chastain.

> *Paris*
> *Tuesday, the 29th of October 1878*
> *Dear Maître de Chastain,*
>
> *I thank you most warmly for the significant role you have played in enabling me to reclaim the two paintings to which I attach such great value. They are now safely in my possession, unscathed by their journey from Provence. Though I have already thanked her, please convey my gratitude once more to Madame Mareuil, without whose help and support my encounter with Madame d'Aurevalle would have been unbearable and my journey to Provence unsuccessful.*
>
> *Through the generosity of my father and mother, I have now acquired my own apartment near Notre-Dame. It is large enough to have my library and the paintings together in one room. The apartment is my kingdom, to which I own the keys and to which I admit only those who have earned my trust. Because of your kindness and concern, you will be one of the few permitted to cross the threshold, should you ever come to Paris again.*
>
> *With my most cordial wishes,*
> *Anne-Sophie Courcel*

He briefly acknowledged my letter and several months elapsed before I heard from him again. In the intervening period, I wrote in my exercise books almost every day, filling page after page with observations, thoughts, feelings, memories. I often went to the theatre with friends. There one evening I met a pretty young actress named

Juliette. She introduced me to her artistic circle, whom I found refreshingly vivacious and disregarding of convention. When she was not rehearsing, we would spend time together discussing the likes of Molière and Racine, just as Célestine and I once had. I enjoyed her company and over the weeks we became closely attached to one another.

One evening, early in 1879, she came to my apartment after a performance, visibly upset.

"Juliette, what is the matter?"

"Fernand. He no longer loves me. He was the only one who did and I still love him. I am heartbroken. I don't know what to do. I don't want to be alone."

"Stay here with me. You can have my bed."

"No, Anne-Sophie. Let us share your bed. I couldn't bear to sleep on my own."

So we lay side by side, just as young children do. Tearful, she asked me to put my arm around her, to keep her safe. I did so. Having Juliette beside me brought back many memories of the times Célestine and I had been physically close and intimate. I found it hard after being alone for so long.

She woke in the early hours.

"Thank you, Anne-Sophie. May I stay with you for a while?"

"Yes, of course you can."

For the next few weeks, Juliette was my companion. Sometimes I didn't see her for several days but I was always happy when she returned. We laughed and acted scenes from plays. We continued to sleep in my bed. I asked if there was any prospect of reconciliation with Fernand. She said there was none – he was now with an older woman. Good riddance to Fernand.

A week or so later, she returned after another of her absences from Paris. That evening, holding my hand, she told me with pleasure of where her company of actors had been. She paused.

"There is something I have to tell you," she said.

"And what is that?"

"I have successfully auditioned for a part in one of Molière's plays. We will perform in Geneva and Lucerne. We will be away for several weeks. Anne-Sophie, please come with me. Let us not disrupt our friendship."

"Juliette, I have several things I must do in Paris in connection with my writing. If I can find the time, I will visit you. I promise."

We talked about her plans late into the night. As we prepared for bed, she kissed me – a long passionate kiss.

"Anne-Sophie, I have a secret to confess."

"If it's a secret you feel you must confess, perhaps you should go to Confession."

"No, it's not that kind of secret. It's a secret about you."

"About me? Surely not," I protested. "Besides, secrets are to be kept, not revealed."

"I'm going to blurt it out. Don't shun me after I have done so. If you were to do that, you would break my heart."

"Juliette, don't be so dramatic. Let us talk about other things. Tell me about your role."

"Anne-Sophie, I have fallen in love with you. That is why I want you to come to Switzerland – to be with me so I may love you, so you may love me."

I didn't know what to say. The words I finally uttered were stilted, unkind.

"Juliette, I am deeply touched by your confession. We have become dear friends. I enjoy your company. But I am not the person you should love. Not long ago you were in love with Fernand and he with you. The day will surely come when another man will take his place in your close affections, giving you the happiness you so deserve."

"It may have been the case then – that he and I loved each other, or at least I thought we did. But that is no longer so. It is you, beautiful Anne-Sophie, whom I love. Can't you see that?"

"Juliette, I am at a loss. Forgive me. If I say more, I will hurt you. That is not what I want to do. I admire you, I am fond of you, but I cannot say I love you."

Juliette's reply struck deeply.

"You have locked yourself away for too long. I know what Célestine meant to you – what she still means to you. You speak of her often.

But the room in which you write, full of paintings to remind you of her, is a mausoleum. It represents the past, self-imprisonment. You are young, like me. You are beautiful and when we've been out walking or at the theatre I have seen how men turn their heads to look at you. But you look away and when you return home you retreat to your room as though to apologise to her ghost. Anne-Sophie, I am the present and the future. I love you and I want us to be together, as you were once with Célestine. It may take time for you to love me as I love you. I will be patient, but do not turn me away."

Her words had wounded me.

"Juliette, you are most welcome to stay here until you leave for Geneva and if you have nowhere else to go on your return to Paris you will be most welcome to stay again, until such time as you find a place that will give you more peace and better hope for the future. As for your feelings for me, I am deeply touched but the matter is closed."

That night we slept side by side once more but there was now a vast emotional distance between us. In the weeks before her departure, I sensed we were becoming competitive, Juliette through her acting and me through my writing. We became secretive and mistrustful of one another. During the day when she was rehearsing or of an evening when she was performing, I would go through her valise to see what she may have written or was reading. I made sure my writing room was always locked when I went out in case she rifled through my exercise books. When we were together and she asked me to test her lines, I sometimes reprimanded her sharply for her lack of concentration instead of giving her gentle encouragement. I began to realise that I was becoming obsessive about her, just as Émile de Beaudreau had become obsessive about me.

The day came for her departure for Geneva. I went with her to the Gare de Lyon and stayed with her until the train left. Our final goodbye was brief, our kisses the conventional one on each cheek. On my return to my apartment, I found a letter from her.

> *My dearest Anne-Sophie,*
>   *I thank you for giving me a home, a place of refuge during the past months.*

*I am not clever with words like you but I wish you to
know that, whatever you may say and however much you
may push me away, I truly love you and it breaks my heart
to say goodbye. I do not know what the future holds for me
but you will always be in my thoughts. I hope that
sometimes you will think of me.*
  Juliette

Her letter pierced my heart. How unkind, how mean-spirited I
had been. For days thereafter I wrote page after page trying to
rationalise everything that had happened in the past years. But the
insight and peace of mind I sought from writing escaped me. I felt
cursed. Should I go to Geneva to see her, to apologise, to embrace her?
Or should I let the waters close over me, releasing me from my
entombing, isolating grief?

As I pondered these dark thoughts, Maître de Chastain wrote to say
that in two weeks' time he would be in Paris to appear in court on
behalf of a defendant accused of fraud. He was confident he would
secure an acquittal and, once he had done so, he intended to stay in
Paris for a few days. He hoped we might go to a musical performance
and perhaps dine together.

Paris
Thursday, the 20th of March 1879
Dear Maître de Chastain,
  *I greatly welcome the news of your imminent arrival in
Paris. I would be delighted to meet you again and, if you
have the time to spare, warmly invite you to join my family
and me for dinner one evening, so we may thank you for all
that you have done for us.*
  With my most cordial wishes,
  Anne-Sophie Courcel

Within the week I received a reply owning that, though he would
indeed be pleased to renew his acquaintance with my family, it was

also his preference that I should be his guest *à deux*.

He duly came to Paris to stay at the Relais Hôtel du Vieux Paris in the rue Gît-le-Coeur. After his legal work was completed, he met my family. The following evening, he and I dined together. I was apprehensive because it was my first public appearance on the arm of a man since I had seen *Carmen* at the opera with Alexandre de Mercier. As we were shown to our table, heads turned, while other diners leaned forward to whisper. But what I observed was of no consequence to me. We went out together several times, to dine or to go to the theatre, greatly enjoying each other's company. My mother described us as the most handsome couple in Paris and said we were apparently the subject of considerable gossip in the city's social circle. Then the time came for him to leave. I was sorry to see him go but he promised to be back in the city before long to continue our friendship.

In the following days, I thought much about him and responded quickly to his letters, in which he told me about what he was doing and the possibility he might soon become a lawyer in Paris, at long last able to escape provincial Nevers. In my replies I regaled him with the latest gossip in Paris. But I could not put Juliette out of my mind. Although I was happy, I could not bear the thought that her lasting memory of me would be one of pain. I decided to visit her. The theatre company with whom she had toured advised me she was still in Geneva. They gave me her address.

On arrival in the city, I found out where she was acting and bought a ticket for that evening's performance. The fluency of her delivery, her timing, the naturalness of her gestures were impressive. I resolved to go to see her the next day to tell her of my admiration, to apologise for what I had said and to renew our friendship.

It was late afternoon when I called on her. I climbed many flights of stairs to reach the top floor, where I saw the colourful umbrella she had possessed in Paris leaning against the wall. It looked rather battered. I knocked on the door. I heard movement, but no one came. I knocked again. I heard the jangling of keys and her mellifluous voice sing out, "Who is it? If it's you, Bernard, I will be ready in a minute. You're too early to escort me to the theatre."

I heard more scuffling and again the sound of keys. Suddenly, the door opened. There she was. She flung her arms around me, hugging me tightly.

"Anne-Sophie, it's you. I thought I would never see you again." She redoubled her embrace. "Come in, please. I have just this room. It's all I can afford on the meagre fee I get."

"I won't stay long. I don't want to get in Bernard's way."

"That's just my trick to ward off unwanted men who pester me."

We laughed.

Sitting on the rickety bed, we talked. That night, after the play, she and I walked by the lakeside.

"Anne-Sophie, I still love you, even though I know you don't love me."

"I've missed you, Juliette. Give me time. My thoughts are confused. Who knows what may happen? But promise me that as soon as you can end your commitment at the theatre, you will come back to Paris without delay and stay with me. There is much for us to discuss."

"I will," she said. "I will."

We took a taxi back to her accommodation, where we parted; I went on to my hotel. The next day I returned to Paris, having first left a letter for Juliette with the concierge of her lodgings.

> *Ma chère Juliette,*
>
> *I wish to express again my profound regret for the distress I caused you before you left Paris. My words and actions were unforgivable. I cannot criticise others for what they have done to me if I commit the same sin against you.*
>
> *I do not know what the future may hold for us. As I said yesterday, only time will tell. But I do know, now, that never again will I reproach you for your feelings towards me, whatever they may be on your return.*
>
> *With my most sincere sentiments,*
> *Anne-Sophie*

She replied swiftly, saying she would be back within the next month or so and would accept whatever I might say about our friendship.

I had not long been back in Paris when Charles de Chastain returned briefly to the city. Shortly before his departure, he proposed to me. I said I would consider his proposal, which had touched me deeply.

Two days later I wrote to him.

> *Paris*
> *Tuesday, the 17th of June 1879*
> *Mon cher Charles,*
>
> *I am greatly honoured that you should ask me to marry you.*
>
> *I do indeed love you for what you are and represent. I will be your admirer, your supporter, your confidante and your loving companion. But I cannot be your complete wife, meeting your physical needs, just as I know you can never be my complete husband in that sense either. Your desires and mine are often met in other ways. That need be no bar to our marriage. Moreover, I will never be jealous if sometimes you are with others. In a similar way, I hope you would be equally generous towards me.*
>
> *Yet for all intents and purposes we would be husband and wife, in a union of deep friendship and commitment. If that is your wish as much as it is mine, then I accept your proposal with profound pleasure, and we can in due course celebrate our union, which outwardly will appear as the world deems a marriage should be.*
>
> *I am yours devotedly,*
> *Anne-Sophie*

By return of post, he wrote to me in great happiness in similar terms. We agreed that before the year was out, I would travel to Nevers to meet his family and so raise the curtain on our eventual union.

At the end of July, Juliette returned to Paris and came to stay with me. That first evening, I broke the news that Charles de Chastain and I would soon marry and that, until his legal career brought him to the city permanently, I would divide my time between Nevers and my writing in Paris. She received the news with evident emotion, but also with resilience.

"I hope that, despite your marriage, we can still be friends."

"Yes, Juliette, we will be friends. And something more than that. Do you still love me – in the same way and to the same extent you said you loved me before you went to Geneva? I need to know."

"Oh, Anne-Sophie! Of course I love you – not just in sentiment but in a deeper, more physical way. Whatever you do, wherever you go, I will always love you. I know I mean little to you compared with Célestine. You will never know how much heartache I suffered after we said goodbye. What I wrote in my letter was true. My heart was indeed broken. Yet the sorrow I endured has made no difference. I loved you then and I love you now. Nothing has changed."

"Juliette, when I came to Geneva and saw you on the stage, I realised what a fool I had been. I will never forget Célestine and the brutal way she was taken from me. But you were right. I cannot cling to the past. It won't come back – *she* won't come back. I must – finally – step out from the shadows of what has been, create my own part, as if in a play, break free from my own obsession. Seeing you on the stage convinced me this is what I had to do. Then last week, I went to a performance of Mozart's *Requiem*, and I understood that, unless I broke free, unless I became the central character in my own play, in my own story, I risked being burnt in an everlasting fire of profound regret." I took her hand. "I love you, Juliette. But our love must be secret, unspoken to all. For it to be revealed would be to risk scandal. Between us, though, it will know no bounds. If what I propose is acceptable to you, I will be profoundly happy."

"I accept," she exclaimed, without hesitation, and embraced me.

That night we slept together, but for the first time intimately, as Célestine and I had done. The next morning, we dressed, planning our day and the week ahead. As Juliette sat on the edge of the bed in her white slip, the dress she would put on tossed casually beside her – a simple everyday scene enacted without reflection, with trust and candour – I knew that in her I had found a companion uniquely feminine and natural, with whom I could be at ease and share my closest secrets as I had once done with Célestine.

Later in the week, Juliette and I went to the Palais Garnier in the Place de l'Opéra to see Mozart's *Don Giovanni*, with its *Ballet des Roses divertissement*, a love story between flowers and butterflies. I watched enthralled as two female dancers executed a *pas de deux* on a largely empty stage in front of scenery painted to evoke exuberant foliage. The principal dancer wore a pink bodice, deep-cerise roses in her skirt and a headdress of pale pink flowers, while her supporting partner was in yellow, with green sepals over her skirt. Both wore black velvet ribbons around their necks. I hoped their elegance, the precision of their steps, their concord with each other and with the music would symbolise the relationship of trust and harmony Juliette and I would have.

As I lay awake in the early hours, Juliette asleep beside me, I was convinced I had at last broken free from Émile de Beaudreau's malign spell, that I had exorcised his spirit, finally overwhelmed him and his lingering demons – and indeed my own. In my mind, I had conveyed them into the flames of hell to share Don Giovanni's operatic fate.

Early the next day, I embarked on a series of letters: to Charles, proposing a date when I should travel to Nevers to discuss our future, and to my family and friends, announcing that forthwith I would spell my surname Courcelle, to be more in keeping with the ancient Burgundian origin of the name I bore. Later, Juliette came with me to lay flowers on Célestine's grave in a small cemetery on the Île de la Grande Jatte, close to the left bank of the River Seine, some eight kilometres north-west of Paris. It was to this island that Célestine liked to come to paint, before she and I became dear friends, honing the skills so evident later in her beachscape at Honfleur.

Placing the bouquet, a symbolic act of farewell, I felt finally able to put aside into pleasant memory the remaining treasured tie with the past and to shed the burdensome bond epitomised by the scornful, tortured Monique d'Aurevalle. Of course, I would never forget Célestine and our love for one another. Her paintings would continue to hang on the walls of my study for me to look at when I paused in my writing, a reminder of how through her I had discovered my true self. As Juliette and I retraced our steps, arm in arm, passing through the old weathered iron gate of the graveyard back towards the river, I sensed I had at last become the lead character in my own story.

AUTHOR'S NOTE

This novel had two main sources of inspiration: a painting and a person.

One Thursday early this year I went from the Foreign Office for a lunchtime walk, not around St James's Park as I often do but to the National Gallery. In Room 41 I saw Pierre-Auguste Renoir's painting *The Skiff*, completed in 1875.

It depicts two women in a boat on a river, one of them rowing. According to the gallery's description beside the frame, rowing boats, sail boats and steam trains crossing bridges were favourite motifs of the Impressionists, of whom Renoir was one. In this instance, the artist combines all three in an iridescent summer scene. Again according to the label, it was probably painted at Chatou, a suburb on the River Seine to the west of Paris.

The painting intrigued me so much that, returning to my office, I decided to write a fictional story about the two women in the skiff – who they were, what their conversation might have been about and what became of them after that afternoon on the river. And if I was fascinated by what I saw, who else visiting the gallery on that day might have been similarly struck?

The second source was Tommy Nguyen, from the Royal College of Music.

During a discussion one day about another novel, he wondered if I would ever consider including a nineteenth-century Cochinchina element. That period of the area where his family originated (present-day Vietnam) could in his opinion provide not only a rich vein of characters – to some extent the concubine Phuong in the novel is based on Tommy's grandmother, regarded in her lifetime as one of the most beautiful women in Vietnam – but also an exotic backdrop to whatever storyline I might construct. His suggestion appealed both for the reasons he had given and because it would provide an opportunity to set another part of the story in France, then the colonial power. Having already seen and been inspired by Renoir's *The Skiff*, I knew the combination of the two ideas would provide a

framework on which to build a story.
Hence the novel you have read.

Edward Glover
North Norfolk
24 November 2019

ACKNOWLEDGEMENTS

I am deeply grateful to my dear friend Tommy Nguyen, not only for inspiring this story and for his encouragement but also for kindly and patiently reading the final proofs of the book to ensure my depiction of Cochinchina was accurate. He has my profound gratitude.

I also thank Madame Odile Castro, citizen of France and a much-admired close friend in my Norfolk village, who helped me choose suitable names for the French characters in the novel, as well as providing details of streets and arrondissements in Paris. Her assistance was invaluable.

My warm thanks go also to Thomas Eymond-Laritaz, who gave me greatly valued advice about the French legal system in the 1870s and about the history of Parc Monceau in Paris's 8th arrondissement where many of the wealthiest haute bourgeoisie had their town houses in that period.

I am grateful, too, to Nicholas Krasno for his exquisite and highly knowledgeable liturgical contribution, in particular the details of the Second Vespers in honour of Saint Andrew the Apostle in the Church of Saint-Sulpice in November 1877.

My gratitude goes, as it always does, to Jenny Langford for once again patiently reading the raw draft of each chapter, correcting typing mistakes and for helping me with some of the research. Her contribution has once again been inestimable.

I also convey my warmest thanks to Sue Tyley, my wonderful copy-editor, who once again applied her highly professional expertise to my manuscript.

Last but certainly not least, I send my special thanks to Niall Cook, my graphics expert, for the design, presentation and production of this book and its cover. Once more, I owe much to his skill and patience.

ABOUT THE AUTHOR

Edward Glover was born in London. After gaining a history degree followed by an MPhil at Birkbeck, University of London, he embarked on a career in the British diplomatic service, during which his overseas postings included Washington DC, Berlin, Brussels and the Caribbean. He subsequently advised on foreign ministry reform in post-invasion Iraq, Kosovo and Sierra Leone. For seven years he headed a one-million-acre rainforest-conservation project in South America, on behalf of the Commonwealth Secretariat and the Government of Guyana.

With an interest in 16th- and 18th-century history, baroque music and 18th-century art, in 2012 Edward was encouraged by the purchase of two paintings and a passport to try his hand at writing historical fiction.

Edward and his wife, former Foreign & Commonwealth Office lawyer and leading international human rights adviser Dame Audrey Glover, now live in Norfolk, a place that gives him further inspiration for his writing. He is vice-chairman and director (communication) of the Foreign & Commonwealth Office Association, a trustee of the Welsh environmental charity Size of Wales and of the King's Lynn Preservation Trust, and an associate fellow of the University of Warwick's Yesu Persaud Centre for Caribbean Studies.

When he isn't writing, Edward is an avid tennis player and completed the 2014 London Marathon, raising £7,000 for Ambitious about Autism.